FROM DENIAL TO DESIRE

A HISTORICAL REGENCY ROMANCE NOVEL

ABBY AYLES

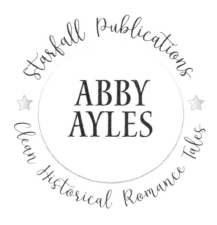

GET ABBY'S EXCLUSIVE MATERIAL

Building a relationship with my readers is the very best thing about writing.

Join my newsletter for information on new books and deals plus all these free books:

- My first published novel - The Duke's Secrets
- My first co-written novel with a famous author and a friend of mine Fanny Finch - The Deceived Lady
- And many more

You can get your books for free by signing up here.

http://abbyayles.com/free-gift

FROM DENIAL TO DESIRE

PROLOGUE

THE MAXWELL ESTATE always caught the eye of anyone who traveled through the countryside around York because it was so grand, so beautiful, and occupied a picturesque piece of land that looked particularly gorgeous in the glistening winter snow. The architecture was beautiful, just like the John Nash buildings that were often admired in London.

Arthur knew that his father, Duke Edward Maxwell, was extremely proud of his home, not just because of the gorgeous stained-glass windows and the turrets that pierced the sky, but because of the fertile land surrounding it. Fertile land that had allowed the duke to live such a lavish way of life.

Now his land had captured the attention of the King, which Arthur was sure his father had orchestrated very deliberately. The duke desperately wanted the King's attention. He saw it as a of achievement to be noticed. He had barely stopped talking about it ever since it happened, and breakfast this morning was no different.

What used to be a quiet affair between the two gentlemen had taken a very different turn today.

"The barley production is making us a *lot* of money," Edward reminded Arthur, as if his son could ever forget. "And it is only going to get better if all my plans come into play. My business plans are going incredibly well. I am very pleased with the way everything is progressing."

"I see that," Arthur replied wryly, not that his father picked up on it. "You have discussed it with me many times recently."

"Well, I do think it might be time for you to start taking more of an interest in what I am doing, business-wise. Since it will all be going to you eventually."

Arthur stiffened. *That* was *not* where he wanted the conversation to go this morning. "I do not know if that is what I want to do with my life."

Edward narrowed his eyes at his son. "Why would you turn your back on a successful business that I have spent my entire life building? Who do you think I have been doing it all for? It is for *you*. To give you a good life."

Arthur gritted his teeth together. There was no point in arguing with his father about it, because the duke really did believe that money was the key to a good life. He did not seem to think that a boy like Arthur might need more.

If his mother had not passed away when he was a young boy, who knew how Arthur's life would have turned out? He was sure his environment would have been more loving if he had grown up with the woman who had given birth to him. What a shame she'd died. He *hated* the fact that she'd died.

"Arthur, you must remember that I will one day be too old to oversee operations. So, then you will have to take the reins. It will be your turn then to be the man you have been raised to be. As a marquess, that is your duty."

"You could always hire someone," Arthur replied. He did not think he was being rude, just speaking his mind. "Someone with the sort of business mind that you have. I would not want to do anything to destroy what you have built up."

Edward's lips thinned into a tight line. Anger bubbled up inside of him, but Arthur knew him well enough to know that he would not let his rage out. He had spent far too many years honing his emotions and keeping them inside for that.

But Arthur would be receiving a lecture. That much was certain.

"You are twenty-five years of age, Arthur. Why can you not be more serious?"

"I am far too busy to run the barley production... ."

"And what are you doing exactly, may I ask?" Redness stained Edward's cheeks. "What keeps you so busy that you cannot take over the business that has been created for you? I do not think you are aware of how lucky you are."

Arthur dropped his spoon in his bowl. It clanged loudly. "I do understand, but I am not sure that barley is where I would like my focus to be. I might be twenty-five years of age, but I do not know what my purpose in life is."

"I have just handed you a purpose in life, Arthur. I have handed it to you on a plate," Edward replied with obvious frustration lacing his tone. "Why must you make it so challenging? You are complicating something that does not need to be complicated."

Arthur sighed sadly and hung his head low. There was something he needed to get off his chest, even if it was not the right time. "I wonder if that has something to do with my mother's untimely death. I lost half my identity then, and I have spent my whole life trying to find it."

Edward's whole demeanor changed. But Arthur was expecting the coldness; his father always became that way whenever Arthur brought up his mother. Edward clearly did not like speaking about his late wife.

"Well, I am terribly sorry about that," Edward said snippily. "But you know your mother was deathly ill. There was nothing that could have been done about it. Yellow fever cannot be helped. It is terminal."

Arthur cocked his head to one side. "And how did she contract it?"

That was something he had never understood. How his mother had gotten the disease. It did not make sense to him, and Arthur was never sure why not.

"She contracted it from a British soldier. There were many soldiers in our social circle." It was always the same story. Arthur knew that very well. Yet he needed to hear it again. "After the bloodletting failed, she simply went downhill, and there was nothing they could do."

Whenever they touched on this subject, Arthur's father always pointed out how pale her skin had been before she died. Arthur thought it would not do him well to point out that the duke himself was looking paler by the day.

"The doctors truly could not help?"

"Bloodletting is the only known treatment for yellow fever in England. You do not think I would have afforded anything I could for her? She was my wife."

Why did his words on this topic always feel so defensive? That might have been why it made Arthur so suspicious. Because it always seemed as if his father became annoyed because he was trying to hide something.

But what could it be? What could his father be hiding?

"I was not trying to suggest that you would not have helped. . . ."

"Good, because Arthur, that is what I did. I tried to help your mother, and it made me terribly sad when I lost her. It has been very hard. *Life* has been very hard since. If there was anything that could have been done, it would have been done, but there was nothing. There was nothing to be done."

Nothing they could do . . . those words made Arthur's heart sink. He might have only been a child at the time, but he wished he could go back in time and assist his mother. Or at least be with her during the hardest time in her life. There were so many things he wished he could have said to her. . . .

Just having that time might have helped him feel less lost in this world.

"Anyway, this might change your mind, Arthur," Edward continued, changing the subject in a heartbeat, something he always did. "I have not yet shown you the letter I have received from the King, have I? You will enjoy it. The King has expressed his admiration for our estate and our barley production. He actually wishes us to expand our empire, to increase production."

"And just how will you do that?" Arthur demanded. "There is no space. Every part of our land that can be used for barley production is already being used for it."

He really could not imagine any other place for planting. If there was one thing he did know about barley, it was that planting too much in one place would end up exhausting the land and killing all the crops.

"Why, I must acquire more land, that is all." Edward beamed. "Once I have the land, I will be able to make a deal with the King. Everything will be perfect. I am sure I will be offered more estates, and I will be able to expand my power."

"How do you intend to acquire the extra land?"

"I always have my ways. That is not something you should worry about." Edward rose from his chair, indicating the conversation was over. "What you need to focus on is the inner workings of the business. Since you *will* be taking over."

"Is that not a part of the business? Should I not know about it too?"

Edward glared at his son. "I will tell you exactly what you need to know when you need to know it. And I do that from a place of care. I do this because I know what is best for you. One day you will thank me."

Arthur was happy for his father, but he could not force joy from his heart. Barley production did not interest him. He could not find it exciting.

Nor did his father's way of doing business excite him. He could not thank him for the business because it was not what he wanted for his life.

He might not have known exactly what it was he *did* want, but he was sure it was not barley production. It was not business either. Certainly not the way he had seen it done for his whole life. It did not fit his personality or desires; it was not something he wished to take upon himself.

Arthur was sure he must take after his mother because he was nothing like his father. That was probably why he struggled so much with his lack of identity. He wanted to know if his mother had also found his father greedy, and far too obsessed with work, money, and trying to impress other people.

Perhaps that was normal for a man with a title. His father certainly acted as though it was the typical behavior of a man of his standing, but Arthur could never picture himself in *that* place. Even if it was expected of him.

As his father stormed out of the room, Arthur swallowed hard. The older he got, the harder his father was on him. Arthur knew it was only going to get worse.

CHAPTER 1

ELLEN'S SOAKING wet hair dangled down her back, stream water still dripping onto her skin. Not that she minded because it helped to cool her down from the intense heat that wouldn't stop burning from the ball of fire in the sky.

It was not often the English countryside was graced with such heat, even in the summertime, so Ellen was not going to complain about it. She tossed her head back and smiled up to the sky, enjoying the feel of its warmth on her pale skin.

"I do not understand you, Ellen," Gracelyn continued, her berating attitude just about the only thing that could wreck such a lovely day. Why she could not simply let the argument go, Ellen could not understand. "I believe you know that you are being far too choosy when it comes to a possible marriage to the consul. I honestly am not sure what you expect. . . ."

"I am not being choosy," Ellen insisted, trying to keep her tone level. The last thing she wanted was for the argument to escalate. It seemed as if Gracelyn really did want to fight. "That is not it at all. I am simply being fair."

"Fair?" Gracelyn scoffed. "How, pray, are you being fair?"

"I simply do not think it fair to marry the consul for his status and nothing else. It may not be a popular opinion, but I truly believe that marriage should be based on love and romance, not practical gain and greed. . . ."

"That is the stuff of fairy tales," Gracelyn snapped, more annoyed about it than she really needed to be. "The reason that is not a popular opinion is because it is a ridiculous one. You must be more practical. As a woman. . . ."

"As a woman, should I just take whatever is offered to me?" Ellen asked, shaking her head to herself. "I should not have any wants or desires of my own?"

"I agree." Ellen's youngest sister, Joy, raced to catch up with her sisters. For some reason, she was always much slower after a swim. It was almost as if the water clogged up her joints and made it more challenging for her to walk. "I do not think anyone should marry for anything other than love. Convenience is not a good reason. Love is the only thing that makes life worthwhile."

Gracelyn scoffed with derision. "See, Ellen? Now you have Joy living in a fantasy land as well. We must marry for money, to ensure we have good, secure lives. You believe you will still be happy with a gentleman who sweeps you off your feet when you are living in a gutter, dressed in rags."

"Oh, why do you have to see it as one way or the other?" Ellen giggled. "Why does love have to equal a life of misery? This is why I do not want to rush into any kind of decision because I am certain I will eventually find my happily ever after."

"See? A fairy tale. You two are asking for trouble. A happily ever after? I do not think either of you are going the right way for that."

"So, what do you want with marriage?" Ellen decided to take a different tactic, to try and get through to her sister. To try and find some common ground with her, so they could build a proper conversation. "What is your plan?"

"I shall marry someone who can give me a good life," she immediately shot back. "Love can grow from that. Love can be formed, but wealth cannot."

Ellen smiled and turned to her middle sister. "Father is very supportive of my decision. He would prefer me to marry for love. You know this... ."

"Father is too kind to tell you that he needs the money." Gracelyn shrugged her shoulders. "He has a lot of stress on his shoulders, which he does not need. Money could help to solve all of those problems, which I believe you know."

Ellen was taken aback with this comment. Her father was always a little tense about money, but she did not believe he would ever push her towards something she was not happy about. Especially when it came to romance and the rest of her life. She did not agree with her sister that love could grow; that was not how she saw her own romance going. She assumed it would be more of a love at first sight kind of thing. She would just know the moment she saw the gentleman.

That was how her father said he'd found the love of his life. Unfortunately, her mother passed away in childbirth with her youngest sister, so Ellen would never hear the other side of the story.

The way Ellen imagined it; it must have been lovely. Their eyes met across a dance hall, and they just knew their lives had changed forever, that they were going to get married and have a lovely life together.

At least, they had enjoyed their lives together until her mother's death.

It was a real shame that her father had lost his soul mate, the one woman he would always love. He was such a wonderful man, and he did not deserve that. It made Ellen so sad, which was why she never wanted to upset him or make his life any harder, making Gracelyn's accusation rather cruel.

"I think you are being a little callous, Gracelyn," Ellen finally told her tautly. "And insensitive as well. Just because we have a differing opinion, does not mean we have to disagree and fall out because of it."

"But your opinion affects me. It affects all of us as a family. That is why I would like you to rethink everything you are doing. It is not just you who must be considered."

Gracelyn stepped quicker, moving in front of her sisters to get away. That was clearly going to be the end of the conversation. More than that, Gracelyn could move faster, knowing she had left Ellen behind with a whole lot of thoughts to try and digest.

Perhaps her sister's colder way of viewing the world was correct. Just because Ellen did not like it, did not mean she assumed it was completely wrong. There were some things she had said which really made Ellen think. She did not wish to affect other people badly with her decisions. Especially not her family. Ellen would do anything for her family, and she desperately wanted each of them to have a nice life... .

But was she willing to marry someone simply for his money?

It was with a truly heavy heart that Ellen continued her journey to the Greenfield home. Even as Joy slipped her hand into hers and laced her fingers through her sister's, Ellen did not feel better. There was a deep weight pressing down on her chest that would not go anywhere.

Gracelyn had her all tied up in knots and very upset. Ellen knew she had a lot of big decisions to make, and things might not turn out the way she wanted.

"Father!" Ellen found her smile once more as she spotted her father, sitting in the parlor with his paperwork as he smoked. "I thought we agreed that you would stop smoking."

"We did not agree on a thing," her father replied with a cheeky glint in his eye. "You have told me that I should quit smoking, and I have agreed that I should. However, as I have explained to you, it is much easier said than done. I simply do not have the willpower to stop. It is terribly unfortunate."

Ellen grabbed on to her father's shoulders from behind and swung around to playfully peck him on the cheek. Her sisters had already raced up the stairs to wash up and get dressed after their swim, leaving Ellen alone to show her father affection.

"How was your swim this morning?" he asked as he put his paperwork down to offer his daughter his full attention.

"It was refreshing. Very nice." Ellen glowered a little. "But I did not much care for the conversation on the way back."

"Oh dear," her father chuckled. "You girls are fighting again? May I ask what it is about this time around?"

Ellen shook her head. She probably should not have let those words escape her lips. It was not right to put more strain onto her father. Especially if Gracelyn was right.

She could not see it in her father's eyes, but perhaps he was well adjusted to hiding his worry from her. If money truly was an issue that only her marriage to the right man could solve, then perhaps it was time for her to stop being so selfish.

Ellen had never considered herself a selfish person. She had prided herself on putting everyone else first, but her conversation today had her reconsidering everything.

If only things weren't so fraught with Gracelyn, then she could ask her.

Ellen's eyes traveled towards the stairs, up which her sisters had disappeared. It would be so easy for her to follow behind them, to perhaps try and straighten things out with Gracelyn and even continue their earlier conversation.

But Ellen did not fancy that idea. She was not quite ready for that conversation just yet. She would much rather avoid it for as long as she could.

"Father, do you maybe have time to put your paperwork and smoking to one side for a while and come for a walk with me? The sunshine is absolutely glorious, and I would love to make the most of it while it is here."

Her father pulled a slightly uncertain face, before nodding and agreeing with his daughter. Thankfully, as dedicated he was to keeping things running smoothly, especially with his business, he was always willing to put everything to the side to spend some time with any one of his girls. Ellen had a feeling he wanted to make up for the fact they did not have a mother around.

If that was his aim, then he had done a very good job of it. Much as the girls all missed their mother, their father had done all he could to bring them happiness every single day.

"Yes, let us take a walk," he declared with a deep warmth to his voice. "It really is a lovely day. I would like to get warm before I do any more work."

CHAPTER 2

PHILIP GREENFIELD WALKED CLOSE to his daughter as they both enjoyed the glorious sunshine for a moment, the silence between them comfortable and happy. The stress that had been coursing through Ellen's veins only moments before while she was with her sisters had dissipated. Her father had helped her with that.

"Oh, my goodness," Philip said suddenly, shaking Ellen from her very peaceful moment. "Look at that. Look at the way the land has started to deteriorate."

Ellen swallowed back her sadness at her father's comment. She knew how hard it was for him to see his beautiful estate leave behind its glory days, but it was an unfortunate thing that simply could not be helped.

As the Greenfield family's wealth had slowly deteriorated, her father had been forced to let servants go, which, of course, led to less work being done. Her father could only do so much. She did not blame him for not being able to do it all; Ellen only wished he would stop taking himself to task about it.

"Do you remember when we used to have a flower garden there?" Philip said wistfully. "And fertile land with lots of space to grow whatever we wanted. It was so beautiful then. I miss the days when we had beauty here."

"What are you talking about, Father?" Ellen laughed, trying to make him feel better. "It is still very beautiful here. Just because it does not look the same as it always used to is not a bad thing. You should not feel shame."

"How do you know I am feeling shame?" he asked, trying to make a little joke out of the comment. "I am not that easy to read, am I?"

"You get a little vein popping in your forehead," Ellen replied. "Right here."

As Ellen twisted around to point to her father's forehead, she saw such a grave expression on his face, it stopped her in her tracks. Her finger remained hanging in the air as she ran her eyes over his face.

"You do know that I love you and your sisters very much?"

"Y . . . yes," Ellen stammered as her hand fell to her side. Why was her father saying *that* so suddenly? Was it because of the fight she'd had with Gracelyn earlier? She hadn't told him the details, and besides, their little spat was nothing serious.

"You girls are my entire world. I do not know what I would do without you."

"Father, that is lovely to hear," Ellen replied with a genuine smile, "but what has made you so sentimental this morning?"

Philip leaned forward and coughed. It was a strained sound, as if his lungs were struggling. It was a sound Ellen put down to his smoking. That was why she did not like his terrible habit; it could not be good for his body.

Finally, he stopped coughing and glanced up at Ellen. "I simply do not say it enough, that is all. It is something I should tell you more often."

Ellen nodded slowly. She wished she could accept that as an explanation, but something about it did not sit right with her.

"Father, statements like that scare me."

"They do?" Philip furrowed his eyebrows. "Why is that?"

"Because when a character in a novel makes a sweeping statement of love like that, it is because one of them is about to die."

Philip was silent with shock for a beat too long before laughter exploded from him, booming from his stomach.

"Oh, my goodness, Ellen, you are such a sweetheart. Honestly, you are so lovely. But you have always spent too much time reading romantic literature. It has shaped your view of the world."

That sounded a little like what Gracelyn had just said to her. That she had her head in books.

"Oh, you do not need to look so horrified, Ellen," Philip insisted. "That is not what I mean. There is nothing wrong with reading."

"But my view of the world—"

"Your view of the world is wonderful. You truly have a special mind."

Ellen softened, and she let out a little laugh. She did not mind being seen in that way by her father because he loved her more than anything in the world, except her sisters, of course, and he was her best friend.

It was a relief when he joined in with her. They laughed together, until suddenly, Philip's facial expression changed completely. He looked las if some horror had struck him, his hand clutching his chest, and the laughter became another sound completely. Instead of laughter, his face became a picture of panic as he wheezed desperately, trying his hardest to gasp for air.

"Father—" Ellen begged, her blood running ice cold. "Father, what is happening?"

He tried to answer her but could not get any words out. Ellen had no idea what was blocking his airway, nor did she know what to do to help.

"Father, what can I do?" His skin paled, his eyes darkened. "Father?"

Ellen trembled. She wanted to reach out and touch her father, but she could not seem to make herself do it. She might as well have been frozen to the spot. The only thing that seemed to be working was her voice, so she had to use it as best she could. Ellen sucked in a deep and shaky breath before screaming at the top of her lungs. "Help! Someone help me. Help me!"

She screamed until her voice was hoarse. Ellen was frightened that her voice would go before anyone would hear it, so she was flooded with relief to hear racing footsteps finally coming towards her.

"Ellen, Father," Joy cried out as soon as she was within earshot. "What is wrong?"

"Joy, we must have a doctor at once!" Ellen called back breathlessly. "We need a doctor. It is Father, he needs medical assistance."

All the color drained from Joy's cheeks as she took in the scene and understood what was happening. Thank goodness she had it in her to nod and spin on her heels. She ran away as fast as she could manage.

"Father, Joy has gone," Ellen said as he sank to his knees. She went down to the ground with him, unable to leave him alone. "She has gone to get a doctor, so you just need to hold on until then." He said nothing, simply continued to stare at her with glassy eyes. "Father, stay with me. Do not slip away from me. I need you."

She thought about the words her father had spoken to her only moments before. She had not truly meant it when she commented about death, but now that whole conversation had taken on a brand new, terrible meaning.

No. She shook her head hard. *No, no, no.*

That could not happen. She could not let it happen.

"Please, Father, do not die. Please do not die." She cradled him close to her, glad she could finally touch him because at least that allowed her to feel she was helping him in some way. "I need you, Father. Do not die."

Where was the doctor? He was needed immediately—now—before things became really dire.

The parlor had never been so painfully quiet, but Ellen did not know what to say, and she was sure her sisters felt the same way. Any arguments that had been boiling over only a short time before were now at the back of their minds.

Ellen reached out to hold Gracelyn's hand. Gracelyn then did the same for Joy. It was unlikely to make any of them feel better, but at least they were not alone. They were sharing the pain together.

Pain Ellen seriously hoped would not last much longer.

If only she and her sisters had not been sent away from her father's side. Why had the doctor done that? She could have helped. She wanted to help. In fact, why was she simply sitting around in the parlor uselessly? That was not what Ellen wanted. Perhaps this was the right moment for her to storm back outside and insist on being close to her father to make sure he was all right?

"Is that the doctor?" Joy whispered, shattering Ellen's grandiose plans before she ended up doing something silly. "He is coming."

Ellen dropped her sister's hand almost as fast as she had grabbed it. As the eldest sister, she needed to be the one there to greet the physician; she had to take charge. Even if she did not want to . . . and was not ready to.

Oh no, she thought desperately to herself. He looks grave.

The doctor's expression was pinched and unpleasant. He had a heaviness to him which followed him into the parlor. Ellen did not like it one bit.

"I am sorry to tell you this—" the doctor said morosely, his arms folded across his front and his head down. He could not meet their eyes. "There was nothing I could do. I'm afraid your father has passed away from a heart attack."

As Ellen took in those words, the world seemed to slip away from underneath her. She did not even realize she was falling to the floor until her hands slapped on the ground and tears splashed upon them.

The doctor continued to talk to the girls, but Ellen was truly lost in an abyss of agony. She had never experienced pain like it before in her life. Her mother might have passed away, but Ellen was too young to have really felt it. Plus, she had still had her father, her best friend, there to look after her.

But now she had nothing; she had no one. She was completely alone.

Well, Ellen had her sisters, but, of course, she was going to be responsible for them. At only twenty-two years of age, Ellen was going to be responsible for everything. Something she was definitely not ready for.

She was drowning, sinking in a deep sea of loss, in pain and horror. It was a cesspit of agony she was sure she would never be able to climb out of.

Life as she knew it had just come to a terribly abrupt end.

CHAPTER 3

THIS WAS NOT A PLEASANT JOURNEY. Arthur would have rather been anywhere else in the world than on this carriage ride to York with his father, to visit the Greenfield estate. But Edward had been determined that Arthur was going to learn the business, and thrive within it, whether Arthur wanted it or not.

Not that a trip across a bleak landscape, drinking in the remnants of what was once a thriving estate but had now been reduced to an eerie ruin, should be about business. Not when the patriarch of the Greenfield family had so recently passed away. But that was Arthur's father; everything was an opportunity, including grief.

There was definitely grief here. Sadness hung over the Greenfield land like a morning fog. With every breath Arthur took, he could feel it filling up his lungs. It was an all too familiar feeling that did nothing to settle the churning in his stomach.

Anything related to death of, course, had Arthur pondering, thinking back on the death of his own mother. This present feeling felt so much worse because she had been on his mind such a lot recently. He did not want the children of this family to suffer the same pain he had been going through for so long.

"Is the mother of the family going to be all right?" Arthur asked quietly.

Edward stared at him. "Do you not recall me telling you? The matriarch of the family passed away whilst giving birth to her youngest daughter."

"Wait—" Arthur gulped. "So, it is only the children left behind?"

This was horrible. His heart sank. It did not matter how young the children were, if they were still living at home and not married, then the loss of their one remaining parent was going to be dreadful for them.

Theirs must be a grief unlike anything he could even imagine. Even worse than what he had been subjected to. Arthur tried to imagine what doubling his grief might be like, but he could not even picture it.

"Who is left?" he whispered. Arthur so desperately wished he had been privy to this information before agreeing to come on this journey.

But if his father *had* told him, he would not have heard it.

"Three daughters," Edward replied, nonplussed. Clearly, he was not suffering from any sympathy for them at all. "Ellen, Gracelyn, and Joy, I believe their names are, but I suppose that is something to be confirmed when we arrive."

Giving the ladies names only made it that much harder to think about them. It almost gave them faces and hearts that Arthur could not do anything to fix. If he could not repair his own heart after his mother's death, then there was nothing he could hope to do for anyone else. He was hopeless, helpless. It was dreadful.

"Oh, my goodness. They must be so heartbroken." Arthur's chest clenched, his heart actually aching for these people. "I cannot imagine."

"Oh, do not trouble yourself too much with their grief," Edward interjected as he patted beads of sweat off his forehead. "I am sure they are not focusing on their pain. The first thing on their minds will be their current lack of financial stability." He let out a light chuckle. "They will see us coming in like angels of mercy come to rescue them."

He did not understand, did he? Arthur was unsurprised to hear the lack of even a scrap of humanity in his father's words. The man had experienced grief and loss in his life before, having lost of his wife. He should have more heart.

Arthur wished he had not asked any questions of his father. The answers had simply reminded him that his father truly was a heartless man. Even at a time when a person was going through one of the worst times of their lives, the dukes priority was money. His greed overtook everything else. Even during a conversation about grief and loss, he had managed to steer it towards money, wealth, or both.

Arthur might have had a better life had he not been born into privilege, if he had just been given a normal life, where nothing was ever expected of him, and he could just be whoever he wanted to be.

Although, since he had never experienced a life without money, he could not really speak to the troubles that life might have brought him without it. He supposed he should not allow his anger toward his father to grab on to his thoughts and control his emotions.

Considering the way the world worked, without a decent financial background, he doubted he would be awarded the chance to do whatever he wanted. He would have to work to support his family, just to put food on the table.

Just because Arthur did not believe his father to be a good man did not mean he wanted to change his whole life around. Instead, he thought it better to engineer his own behavior to make up for his father's ice-cold attitude towards everything and everyone.

If Edward was going to be cold and calculating, then he himself would show these poor Greenfield girls that they did have the sympathy of his family after all.

"We are here now," Edward declared, stiffening in his seat. He threw his shoulders back and held his head high, needing to show off his power and wealth, no matter what the situation. "We must show these girls we are their saving grace."

Arthur glowered, annoyance rippling through his veins. He knew his father was not thinking about kindness or saving anyone. He wanted the Greenfield's land; he wanted to expand his barley empire, to impress the King, and to increase his own power.

Ever since the King had sent him the letter, it seemed to be all the duke thought about. There might as well have been nothing else in his brain at all.

"Will you sit up straighter?" Edward snapped. "You need to make a good impression. I can already see from here that the girls are waiting for us."

That captured Arthur's attention. Since the girls were drowning in grief, he was not expecting them to be outside the door, ready to greet them. But there they were, heads hung low, expressions somber, the weight of pain clearly resting on their shoulders.

All he could really see was the pain etched in the expressions of the women, who stood in the shadows of a building that looked as if it had been disintegrating for years, with its crumbling walls and a roof which clearly needed a lot of attention. If he had not known people lived here, he might have assumed the entire estate was abandoned.

Much as Arthur did not wish to agree with his father, perhaps his insistence on buying the land was actually exactly what the three sisters needed. So long as his father offered a fair price and did not try to take advantage of the grief the women were suffering, then perhaps Arthur could be content with his actions.

"Good morning, ladies," the duke said in an insufferably arrogant tone as he descended from the carriage. Arthur cringed, embarrassed. "I am sorry we must meet in such unfortunate circumstances."

The three sisters, having been trained to behave in a certain manner throughout their entire lives, greeted the duke in the proper manner. The tallest stepped forwards first, immediately capturing Arthur's attention in a way he was not expecting. This time, it was not just the suffocating sadness that caught his focus. It was her.

She was utterly breathtaking. The most beautiful woman Arthur had ever seen in his life. A mass of rich red hair cascaded down her back, with charming little curls framing the pale, delicate face which rose above a slender, white neck. Her large green eyes sang with pain, but Arthur was sure he saw a glint of iron there. It was almost imperceptible, but it was there. Her slender frame was perfectly set off by the pretty dress of white lace she wore, her figure drawing his eyes.

She was so lovely, Arthur could not catch his breath as he looked at her. He was supposed to be offering the sisters his sympathy, but his brain was immediately clouded by the sight of this woman. She was like an angel sent from heaven. No—she was a goddess. As she introduced herself as Miss Ellen Greenfield, the musical lilt of her voice made his pulse race, something no other woman he had ever met in his life had made him feel.

Even as she stepped back from Edward and her sisters were introduced, Arthur could still not take his eyes away from Miss Ellen. If she sensed his eyes upon her, she did not lift her gaze from the ground. She was too sad, in too much pain. All Arthur wanted to do was jump from the carriage, to hold her in his arms, to make her feel better.

Not that he could do so. Social conventions forbade physical such intimate contact, even in a time of grief, especially between strangers. It was not even something Arthur would normally have even considered. But there was something about Miss Ellen that made him want to throw all his usual rules and behaviors out of the window.

"Arthur," Arthur's father suddenly snapped brusquely, finally dragging him from his thoughts about Miss Ellen. The duke demanded his son's absolute concentration so he could forge ahead with his scheme to buy the Greenfield estate. "Will you please step out of the carriage?"

Arthur felt heat race through his body and rise to his cheeks. He did not want to blush in front of these young women—indeed, he did not feel he had the right to, but unfortunately, he was quite unable to control his body's natural reaction.

He felt embarrassed and awkward, which was not the first impression he wanted to give the women. Especially not Miss Ellen. He wanted to appear sensitive and gracious, to offer her and her sisters his deepest sympathies.

That was not going to be easy with a sense of humiliation surging through his veins. He stepped carefully from the carriage, trying not to lose his footing. The last thing he wanted to do was make things worse by falling at her feet.

CHAPTER 4

ELLEN'S HANDS trembled as she carried the tray of tea and cakes from the kitchen into the drawing room, where their guests were waiting for her.

"Oh, my goodness," Edward Maxwell, Duke of York, exclaimed when he spotted her. "Lady Greenfield, what are you doing, bringing in the refreshments yourself?"

"Father!" the young marquess, Arthur Maxwell, exclaimed, clearly shocked. "How can you ask such a thing?"

Ellen panicked, the last thing she wanted was for these visitors to argue in her home. "No, please, Your Grace, my lord, it is quite understandable to ask such a question." She carefully laid out the tea things on a low table before the gentlemen, needing to concentrate on one thing at a time. Once that was done, she primly took her seat and folded her hands together. "Let me explain, Your Grace. Toward the end of my father's life, our financial situation became quite . . . challenging. Some unfortunate mismanagement, I believe. Many servants were let go out of necessity, so my sisters and I were forced to take on most of the household duties."

"That is a shame," the stern-looking duke replied, shaking his head.

"Oh no, it is no difficulty," Ellen insisted. "We do not mind. And we were always happy to do anything to help our father. Tea, Your Grace? Marquess?"

"Thank you," said the marquess, while his father gave a stiff nod of acceptance.

Ellen sucked in a slightly shaky breath as she poured the tea, trying her hardest to keep her emotions locked away inside. Ellen had done nothing but cry ever since their father passed away, quite bereft without her best friend beside her, but she would never allow herself to show that devastation in front of company, and especially not before such august gentlemen. She had been trained to always behave respectfully toward her betters because that was what a 'lady' did.

"I have never enjoyed it," Gracelyn suddenly blurted out, bitterness evident in her voice.

Everyone turned to look at Gracelyn in shock. Ellen might have been used to Gracelyn's outbursts but that did not mean they were acceptable in front of others.

"Please forgive my sister's forthright manner, my lords; she is deep in grief and not quite . . . herself. Cake, my lords?" The gentlemen assented, and, as she served the cakes, Ellen sent Gracelyn a sharp glance before adding, "Our father was a very good man. A wonderful man. He does not deserve to be poorly judged simply because he made a few mistakes in business."

Ellen noticed that the duke, who was biting into a light, lemon sponge finger, scrutinized Gracelyn closely as he chewed, seeming to sense the tension between the sisters. The sponge was gone in a few seconds, after which he sipped his tea and smiled. It was a smile, Ellen thought, of intense satisfaction—but not, she suspected, for the excellence of the cake. Ellen could not know what was crossing his mind at that moment, but a sense of discomfort flooded her. She shifted in her seat, her eyes fixed upon the old duke, waiting for him to continue with the conversation.

"I do not judge," he eventually replied. "I would certainly not wish to be thought of as judging Lord Greenfield. We were, alas, not well acquainted. My question was merely asked in some surprise at seeing you serve us yourself, Miss Ellen and was perhaps ill-judged. I apologize. I meant no disrespect."

Ellen tried to smile, to let the duke know she accepted his words of apology and had not been troubled by his question. But, unfortunately, she could not do it. There was something about the man she didn't trust. The Duke of York had not done anything overtly to cause the sensation; it was simply something she felt in her bones.

"Knowing a little of your troubles following your father's sad demise —" the duke continued as he rested his teacup in its saucer, "the marquess and I have come to call on you today . . . to offer you ladies our help."

"You wish to help us, Your Grace?" The knot of distrust in Ellen's stomach intensified. "How kind. Pray, how do you propose to help us?"

The duke suddenly beamed from ear to ear, almost wolfishly, Ellen thought. "I would like to make you an offer, one that will ensure your financial troubles are no more."

Ellen's eyes whipped around. Just as she had suspected they would at this, Gracelyn's eyes had lit up with excitement. Fleetingly, Ellen's thoughts returned to the conversation she'd had with her sister before their father passed away—the one about marrying for money. She knew for sure that Gracelyn would do absolutely anything to make sure she had a comfortable life financially. But, as the eldest child, it was Ellen's responsibility alone to make sure that whatever the duke had to offer was right for them all.

She did not want to give up their land, and judging by the suspicion in Joy's eyes, she was not keen on the idea either.

But unfortunately, Ellen knew she might not have a choice in the end. For her sisters' sake, she was at least going to have to hear the man out. Which was why she looked back at the duke once more.

"What kind of . . . offer are you referring to, Your Grace?"

"Well, if one of you were to marry my son, Arthur here. . . ." The duke gestured with his head to his startled-looking son sitting beside him, but Ellen could not move her stunned gaze from the duke's face. ". . .And use your fields as a dowry, then your position would improve immediately. Immeasurably, in fact. Not only that, but I will restore the Greenfield estate to its former beauty and offer you a home at the Maxwell estate, which, as I am sure you know, is one of the finest in England."

Gracelyn gasped. Joy clapped her hands to her mouth. Ellen remained stiff as stone. Had she heard him correctly? The duke's offer involved marriage? That was why he had come? It was the most shocking thing that had ever happened to Ellen. She did not know what to say.

"Father, I did not know—"

The duke held up a finger to silence his son. But it did not matter. The marquess did not need to finish his sentence for his meaning to be perfectly clear to Ellen. This was not what he had expected when coming to the Greenfield estate.

Slowly, agonizingly slowly, she dragged her eyes away from the duke to look at the marquess. She wanted to see the confusion in his eyes, to see how he felt about this . . . *offer*. Ellen felt as if her life had been spiraling out of control ever since her father had said those powerful words: "*You do know that I love you and your sisters very much?*" And now, it did not seem to be getting any better.

Her sisters knew she wanted to marry for love, not convenience. That was what her father had wanted for her, and what she wanted for her sisters as well. Whatever Gracelyn said, Ellen wanted love and happiness above money for her sisters.

As she finally caught the marquess's gaze, she jolted, because he was looking right back at her. His inquisitive gray eyes burned through her in a way she found oddly electric. As he reached up and raked his fingers through his golden hair, a little shiver trickled down her spine.

He was incredibly handsome, she had to admit. With his tall, muscular stature, his strong jaw, and kind eyes . . . he did not seem to be anything like his father, and that intrigued her.

"Lady Greenfield," the marquess finally said, a degree of a tentative curiosity lacing his tone, "I hope you won't mind me saying that I find you very beautiful—"

Beautiful? Ellen rested her hand on her heart. No one had ever called her beautiful before. Well, aside from her father, but he was obligated to say so. The marquess had absolutely nothing to gain from calling her beautiful . . . aside from setting the seal on his father's plans. Although he did not look overly concerned about that, she thought, wondering if she was reading him correctly.

There was a softness to his eyes, to his face, which caused her to melt just a little under the intensity of his gaze. Once the initial shock wore off, she felt a smile creep up onto her face.

She'd noticed that, where the duke had seemed eager to check his reflection in every mirror they'd passed on the way to the drawing room, the marquess seemed much more interested in the world around him. His inquisitive gaze roved over everything in. While the two men had a similar build and the same strong, dark features, that was where the similarities ended.

But the differences were only clear after studying the men carefully.

"You are indeed very lovely, and clearly a very capable lady, too, which I very much respect. I would like to get to know you better," the marquess said with a tentative smile.

Heat shot through Ellen's veins, rising instantly to her cheeks. She averted her gaze from the marquess and toward her sisters. In this unfamiliar situation, they were familiar, and she drew comfort from their presence. She needed that comfort in the face of this handsome gentleman, who was a complete stranger to her but claimed he wanted to get to know her better with, apparently, the thought of marriage in his mind.

Joy, surprisingly for someone who insisted she too wanted a fairy tale romance for herself, looked very pleased for Ellen. She was even nodding encouragingly, as if Ellen should simply agree to the offer immediately. Gracelyn, however, had her head hung low, as if she could not stand to look at her elder sister.

But was this not exactly what Gracelyn said she wanted Ellen to do? Ellen would have almost expected Gracelyn to agree to the offer on her behalf! But now, as the tempting option was put in front of the Greenfield sisters, Ellen thought both Joy and Gracelyn were acting strangely.

"This is something I need to think about," Ellen finally replied. It was the best answer she could give at that moment because she did not know how to respond or what to do.

It was wonderful that this man had called her beautiful. She felt very flattered by the compliment. And the marquess was a truly handsome man. But his father appeared to be money hungry, one who cared much for his appearance, judging by his fancy clothing and the way he held himself, as if he knew he was an incredibly important man. The marquess had the same pale skin, so perhaps he was really as money hungry as his father? Without knowing more about him, Ellen was far too terrified to agree to the offer right away.

The last thing she wanted was to land her small family in an even worse situation than that which they were already in.

The duke nodded slowly and rose to his feet. He did not look too pleased by Ellen's response. "Time is of the essence here," he said firmly. "Of course, you are permitted a few days to make your decision."

He really did expect her to agree right away, Ellen realized. She escorted the pair towards the front door as they politely took their leave, fearing she might be allowing the one and only opportunity the Greenfield girls would have to get out of their terrible situation to slip away.

If only her father were there. He would know what to do.

All the years he had spent telling her to marry for love because that was the only way she could be happy faded away a little now. It did not seem practical when their family was facing ruin and there were no parents around to advise her on such a life-changing decision.

She waved the duke and marquess off with as much composure as she could muster. Then, she shut door on them and leaned against it, almost breathless. While she might have appeared 'capable' to the marquess, the great responsibility crushed her, as its full weight began to settle on her shoulders. There was no father there to make the decisions for her and her sisters. It was all up to her.

So, what did she do now?

Did she allow this marquess to interfere in her life? Merely on the suggestion that they got to know one another, with no promise of marriage at the end of it? He did not seem like such a terrible man with a horrible agenda, but Ellen was still terrified.

Everything really was going to change now. Ellen had known change was coming the moment her father passed away, but now she was really facing the consequences of it. It was a consequence that might take her away from everything she had ever known. How could she accept that with grace?

CHAPTER 5

ELLEN HAD KEPT herself busy for the remainder of the day, ever since the duke and the marquess left the Greenfield estate because she did not know what to say to her sisters. She knew that both Joy and Gracelyn had many questions for her, which currently, she could not answer. Ellen had never been so confused, and she desperately struggled to understand her situation, but it all felt like too much.

So, she had spent far too much time tidying up the parlor, and Ellen had absolutely no intention of stopping until she thought her sisters were fast asleep. Perhaps after a night of rest, everything would be clearer.

"Oh!" Ellen gasped in shock as she spun around to find Gracelyn standing in the corner of the parlor with her arms folded across her chest and a very sullen expression on her face. "Gracelyn, I did not know you were there."

Gracelyn's gloomy temperament filled the whole room, upsetting Ellen even more. Now, she was going to have to face her sister when she really wasn't ready for it.

"Is there something you would like to discuss?" Ellen asked. She knew she would probably not like what her sister was going to say, but she felt it was best to get it over with.

"Yes, there is, actually," Gracelyn snapped. "I would like to know why you continue to be so difficult with every prospect that comes into your life."

"I was not being difficult. I said I would think about the duke's offer."

"You know we are not going to get a better offer than that," Gracelyn snapped back with clear irritation. "The man is a marquess, for goodness' sake! He has a title and a wonderful estate. Do you know where he lives? Have you seen his home? I have not, but it is reputed to be one of the grandest in the country, as the duke said. Surely, it is very beautiful, and they have many other estates too. As the Duke of York, you know they are rich beyond imagining."

Ellen nodded and let her eyes drop to the floor. "You think I do not understand that? I do. But I am troubled by the idea of giving away our estate."

"Oh, you mean the estate that is rotting away, has been rotting away, and is in desperate need of care and money?"

"Gracelyn, you should not talk like that." Ellen shook her head sadly. "You know how hard our father worked to build the estate back up to what it once was."

"What it once was, yes. But what is it now?" Gracelyn gestured towards the door of the house. "It is a shambles out there. Father knew it, and deep down I believe you know it as well. You must be able to see it."

The strain balled up in Ellen's shoulders. How could Gracelyn be so cold about their father? "He put so much love into this estate," she insisted. "Giving it away like this would be discrediting him. I do not take that decision lightly."

Gracelyn snorted with derision. "Our father is not here anymore. The fields are all we have left. Should we cling to them for some sentimental claptrap to the detriment of us all?"

Ellen turned away from her sister to try to gather herself before she responded. Gracelyn seemed to be angling for an argument, and Ellen really did not want to give in. She already had enough on her mind.

"Well, then, maybe I am wrong," Gracelyn finally said, the tightness in her tone loosening a little. "Perhaps the land is not all that we have left of our father. Maybe his spirit is with us always, no matter where we go. He will always be there. Maybe he even sent the duke and the marquess here, to save us from the sinking ship we are left in."

"Sinking ship?" Ellen snapped back. "I do not feel as though we should call our home a sinking ship. Think of everything that has happened here. Our entire family history has occurred in this home. A lot of it happy. I do not know if I am ready to leave that behind, to say goodbye to the place where we have lived so long as a family."

Gracelyn glowered again. "We do not have time to pander to your nostalgia, Ellen. There is nothing wrong with the marquess."

"I agree," Ellen interjected. "He seemed kind."

"So, what is the problem? Why did you not agree to the proposal at once?"

"There was no proposal," Ellen reminded her. "He simply wishes to know me better, that is all. Do not get carried away with yourself."

"You are so spoiled," Gracelyn tutted. "I wish the proposal had been made to me instead because I would have at least appreciated it. I would do whatever is necessary to make sure we do not end up in poverty."

Ellen could no longer contain herself. She had been trying her hardest not to lash out at Gracelyn, but she could not restrain herself any longer. "My decision has nothing to do with marriage. I wish you would stop bringing it back to that."

"Then what is it about?"

"Our father!" Ellen gasped. "This is about what our father spent his entire life working for. He worked hard to earn an honest living. In one conversation with the duke, which lasted less than ten minutes, his livelihood and hard work was put at stake."

Gracelyn fell into silence for a while, but Ellen could still see the cogs ticking around in her brain. She was certain the conversation was not done yet. There was no point in continuing to busy herself in the parlor any longer. It would do no good. Instead, she leaned against the wall and waited for her sister to speak. Which of course, after a little while, she did.

"I know how close you were to Father, Ellen, so I understand this is hard on you. It is hard on all of us, but you especially. And I am sure you must feel uncomfortable with having to make such a momentous decision. But, the fact is, you must. This is not just about your future; it is for all of us."

"I know, but..."

Gracelyn held up her hand to silence Ellen. "But Father is not here anymore. However hard he worked in his life, that is no longer a consideration. We need to think about ourselves and how we are going to look after one another. This is your opportunity to look after *us*. Joy and me. You *cannot* merely brush aside this generous offer for purely selfish reasons."

"I am not being selfish," Ellen growled back. "I cannot believe you could even suggest it. I am trying to decide what is best for everyone."

"No, Ellen, you are not." Gracelyn shook her head hard. "You are not thinking about anyone else. If you were, then you would already be engaged. We would not be having this conversation because instead we would be planning your wedding and thinking happily about how our money troubles are over." Gracelyn clucked her tongue with annoyance. "Instead, here we are, your two sisters. Dependent on you, just waiting for you while you shillyshally for some silly sentimental reason of your own."

With that, Gracelyn spun on her heels and left Ellen behind in the parlor, consumed with sadness. She was torn between utter rage towards her sister, who did not seem to understand her at all, and heartbreak. She was crushed by the situation. She could hardly even stand any longer. Her knees gave way, unable to hold her up.

Ellen slid down to the floor, tears cascading down her cheeks, and she sobbed. Her hands rested on the carpet, and that was where she stayed for some time, weeping in solitude. She was alone. Ellen already knew that; she had known it ever since her father passed away. But now she really felt it.

This was the loneliest she had ever felt in her entire life.

Ellen had spent a lot of time feeling alone, by herself, on the outside looking in. But truly, she had never felt worse, or more afraid.

Guilt, grief, and loneliness swept over her like a giant wave. It was a horrible combination, crushing, debilitating. Ellen was not sure she would ever be able to get up from her place on the carpet because sadness held her captive there, helpless, like a pinned butterfly.

As she lay on the floor crying, she considered finding Joy to talk to her about the situation, to get her other sister's opinion, but she did not move. Ellen had never had to rely on her sisters to confide in before. If she'd needed to speak to someone, it had always been her father. Especially in such an unforeseen, alarming situation, something so important and life-changing.

Eventually, Ellen realized that poor, young Joy did not deserve to have such troubles put on her shoulders. She was only nineteen years of age, which, of course, was only a year younger than Gracelyn, but she was young for her age. She did not cope well with problems. Joy liked happiness and having a nice time. Ellen was not sure her youngest sister had even started to digest the fact that their father had gone. It was the worst thing that had ever happened to Ellen since their mother's death, when she herself had been a mere baby. So, no, Ellen did not want to put anything else on Joy's shoulders. She must deal with it herself.

The decision was Ellen's alone. It was up to her, and her alone. Whatever Gracelyn said, however much she tried to push her in one direction or another, Ellen was the one who must decide on all their futures . . . which depended upon whether she married the Marquess Arthur Maxwell of York, or not.

No, she could not think too far into the future just yet, because it utterly terrified her. But she must decide if she wished to spend any time with this . . . stranger . . . learn something of his true nature. It should not be such a hard choice perhaps, since he had seemed pleasant, and he had called her beautiful. But Ellen's mind was frozen, and she felt completely unable to think clearly. It was not a decision she had ever wanted to make.

What would he think of her? She certainly did not feel her best self, and much as she fiercely denied her sister's accusation of selfishness, Gracelyn's words remained stuck in her brain.

What if she did let the marquess into her life and he ended up rejecting her because she was not the person he thought she was. That would remove any element of choice, but it would not make her life any easier because Gracelyn would never forgive her. She would always hate Ellen for condemning them to endless money worries, possibly even destitution, for the rest of their lives. The argument would never end.

CHAPTER 6

IT WAS A RESTLESS NIGHT. Ellen had spent more of it awake than sleeping, tossing and turning under the sheets while her troubles circled her. The crisp morning air did nothing to ease her mind, as she had hoped it would. Truth be told, poor Ellen still had absolutely no idea what she was going to do.

To still have no answers was troubling. It was confirmation to Ellen that the situation was more serious than she wanted to admit. Even to herself. She had wanted today to be a much easier day, but it seemed as if it was going to be just as hard.

She sighed deeply and leaned on her windowsill, staring out on the fields she so desperately wanted to protect. Her father's fields. Again, she found herself wishing he was there to give her advice on what to do. He would know.

Ellen leaned on her hands, her elbows resting on the sill, and her eyes fell closed. For a second, she drifted back to a time when she could just wake up in the morning and float down the stairs to find her father in his study doing some paperwork, smoking, the sweet smile on his face silently reassuring her that everything would be fine.

No duke, no marquess, no browning fields losing money. Just green pastures and paradise. Back when Ellen's life was perfect and so much easier. With smiles and laughter, fun and joy, her sisters playing, her father watching them from afar, their lands making them plenty of money, so they never had to worry. The home was filled with servants who loved working for the Greenfield family.

It filled her with warmth, reminding her that there was happiness once. If only she could remain back there, where life had been so glorious.

But, of course, Ellen had to open her eyes eventually. She had to wave goodbye to her dreams and face reality once more. The grim reality she did not want to accept. No more green, plush pastures, no more love and happiness. The deep, black sadness swallowed her up whole, the warmth dissipated into nothingness.

Nothing had changed. Her world was exactly the same. Her father was still gone, and Ellen remained stuck in this frightening, horrible place, with the weight of the world pressing down on her shoulders, forcing her to make a choice one way or the other. Not that either of the choices were preferable. She did not want either of them.

"What would he tell me?" she whispered to herself. "What would Father say to me?"

Ellen drifted away from the window to her washbasin because she absolutely needed to wash her face, to wash away the thoughts and sadness of the past few weeks. Not that anything was ever going to rid her of the pain which had settled within her. Without her father around, nothing would ever be the same.

Perhaps washing would also help to clear her brain. Because just then, there was so much fog, she could not see through it.

"Maybe he would tell me to sell the fields," Ellen whispered to her reflection quivering in the water of the basin. "To make sure we girls can be secure financially 'til we marry. We could find somewhere else to live together and never depend on a man again."

That was a laughable thought. If it was not so tragic, she would giggle. Of course, she could not sell the fields and find another home for herself and her sisters. Of course, she could not get through life without relying on a man because the world did not work that way.

Ladies were not allowed to be involved in business. Alone, Ellen would not be able to sell the fields. No man would purchase from her; and even if he did, he would not give her their true worth. She would still end up with nothing, and her sisters would never forgive her for leaving them stranded.

"If only Gracelyn were a brother rather than a sister. That would be better."

Of course, Ellen did not mean it. She had far too many differences with Gracelyn for them to get along well all the time. But for practical reasons, it would have been a lot simpler if one of the Greenfield children were born male. That way, she would not be stuck in this corner she was currently backed into. She would have another way to solve all the family issues without having to take the advice of the duke and Gracelyn.

"Will I really have to do this?" she wondered. "Am I actually going to have to get married to a man I do not even know? That I definitely do not trust. . . ."

Ellen's lips turned down into a frown. Thinking of the marquess unsettled her. She did not yet know how to read him; she could not work out anything about his character. There did seem to be a kind side to him if his eyes were to be believed, but since his father had the air of a ruthless businessman, his son surely had to be the same. From the limited experience Ellen had with members of the opposite sex, sons raised by fathers like that only knew one way of behaving.

The marquess must surely share that same financially focused mind. But not focused on money in the same way as she was having to worry about it just then—as a necessity for survival. No, that type of focus meant putting money above everything else, even family or love. It meant wanting to marry for fields rather than because they had real feelings for their spouse; love did not even matter to them.

It made Ellen sad to even think about a loveless marriage like that. There must be many people who had been forced to suffer that awful institution throughout their whole adult lives, but Ellen never thought she might be one of them. It hurt to think it might be.

Ellen's dreams of what Gracelyn called a 'fairy tale' romance could not be further away from her reality. Everything Ellen had ever wanted was slipping through her fingers like grains of sand. She did not have a chance of holding on to them or grasping them again. It was hopeless, and the realization crushed her.

Love was something Ellen's father had really wanted for her, so going forward with the Maxwell's plan was really just going to be another way of letting him down. Would he be upset with her for making poor choices in the wake of his death? Especially if she did so too quickly. Not that she had been given time to properly think things through.

The ruthlessness of the duke's character showed in the short time he'd given her to give her answer. The pressure he was putting on her shoulders by forcing her to make such an important decision so quickly showed what sort of man he was. He wanted her answer right away, despite its serious import on her life and the lives of Gracelyn and Joy.

Deep down, Ellen knew she did not really have a choice, that there was no other option. If she did not agree to the duke's proposal, what else would she do? How else would she ensure her sisters did not descend into squalor?

She *had* to make the sacrifice for their sakes, even if she hated the thought. Even if it meant she was letting down her father by not doing the one thing he had so desperately wanted for her. One of the final things they had talked about before he passed away... .

Ellen brushed a stray tear from her eyes. She did not have time to cry, she did not have time to give in to the sadness. She did not have time for any of it, not with the deadline so fast approaching. Instead, what she must do was to make her next move.

Or perhaps she simply needed confirmation that she really had no other option—because if there was *anything* else she could do, then Ellen wanted to know what it was.

"I must speak with my sisters," she said aloud. "We must make this decision as a family, all of us together. This does not affect just me. This is about them as well."

As angry as Ellen was with her sister, as hurt as she remained from the argument they'd the previous night, Gracelyn's opinion was valid. Both she and Joy were going to be impacted either way. If Ellen chose not to get married to this man, then they would have to work out a financial plan together, and if she did—

Well, they were going to have to start planning a wedding.

Ellen attempted to get a little bit excited by the idea of a wedding because she had always loved the idea of being a princess for a day, of wearing the gorgeous dress and having a wonderful party where she was the center of attention. That was not something Ellen usually liked; she was more of a wallflower, but on her wedding day, she had always assumed she would be swimming in love.

She'd always thought her wedding day would be the first day of the rest of her life, the happiest she had ever been, a day when she would be looking forward to the rest of her life. But now, if she really did go forward with this plan to marry the marquess, it would not be like that at all. It would be a terrifying day, and she would not enjoy a single second of it. Ellen would not want any eyes on her, she would want it to be over as quickly as possible. With the marquess by her side, she would be heartbroken.

"But this is not about me," she reminded herself. "This is about my sisters as well. I must get dressed and find them before the situation grows any worse. Before Gracelyn gets even more annoyed with me than she already is. She is known to hold a grudge."

But surely, in such dire circumstances, even Gracelyn would not hold a grudge. This was not one of their usual falling outs. This was going to affect them for the rest of their lives, so petty stubbornness had no place in the conversation.

What was Ellen to wear to a meeting like this with her sisters? It felt important. Almost as important as what she was to wear when she was out in public. She wanted both Gracelyn and Joy to know that she was serious about it all. Gracelyn especially.

CHAPTER 7

LONELINESS CLUNG to Arthur like a wet shirt he could not seem to remove however hard he tried. The Maxwell mansion could not have felt emptier if it was truly deserted. The footsteps and hushed chatter of the servants echoing through the hallways seemed far distant, not affecting him at all. He felt completely alone.

What would another gentleman in his position do? Arthur did not know. He knew he was not the only person in his elevated social circle who was unhappy with the decisions made on his behalf. Parental interference was common amongst the *ton*, so there must be plenty of other men like himself, men who did not like the path their parents had chosen for them. It was all about duty, family, and reputation.

Unfortunately, Arthur could not think of anyone to speak to about it. There was no one to ask. He might have had friends in school to confide in about life and the problems that came with it, but that was a long time ago now. They had all moved on with their lives and were no longer in touch.

Perhaps if Arthur had lived the typical life of a gentleman of his standing, things would be different. But he only attended the events he absolutely had to, and when he was at balls and parties and such-like, he engaged with others in the proper manner, as was expected of him. But he never let anyone get close to him. Arthur had always felt different, and that created a barrier between himself and other people. He did not make close friendships.

Normally, that did not bother him, but now, when he needed someone to talk to, it was a hard pill to swallow. How could he get advice with no friends to ask?

As Arthur wandered through the house aimlessly, he passed his father's office. For a second, he paused as if considering going inside.

Ha! That was a joke. His father was not the sort of man to discuss issues of the heart with. Especially if Arthur's emotions might potentially get in the way of his financial dealings. His father was confident that Ellen Greenfield would agree to his proposal. No doubt he was already drafting his letter to the King to inform His Majesty that his loyal subject was on the verge of obtaining more land estined for barley production.

Arthur hated it. He absolutely hated the thought of his father's happiness, when he himself felt as if the poor Greenfield girls were being pushed into a situation they were not happy with. If only his father would take just one step back, he might see that he was putting those poor girls in a terrible spot. He was *not* an angel offering them salvation; he was a devil, taking advantage of the innocent sisters by exploiting their misfortune and pushing them into a corner. Swooping in like a vulture at the worst moment of their lives and making it ten times worse.

Arthur sighed to himself and gave up any thought of trying to persuade his father to change tack. If Arthur even so much as mentioned it, the duke would doubtless either get angry, making him feel guilty for having such feelings at all, or turn the conversation back around to money. The financial benefits of the proposal outweighed anything else in the duke's mind. Especially the feelings of those poor girls—

Passing the drawing room, the marquess spotted two of the maids whispering in a corner of the room, laughing together and sharing a joke. They appeared to be genuine friends, which only made Arthur's heart ache all the more.

The maids caught sight of him watching and jumped away from one another as if struck by lightning. Arthur was not sure why they should do so; he was not his father. He would never shout at them for talking. The only things he felt was pain and increasing sadness.

He averted his eyes and turned away so the maids knew he did not mind their talking. Arthur continued his aimless journey around the house. He was starting to think he might take a walk outside. The weather was not wonderful; there were thick heavy clouds hanging in the sky that had the potential to turn gray at any given moment, but the fresh air might clear his head and help him think.

How do other gentlemen build friendships? he asked himself as he reached the front door and slipped out into the grounds. *Maybe all this is a sign that I need to change my life... .*

But as he thought about it, Arthur started to realize that, perhaps, he was not so strange after all. *Certainly, there is always plenty of talk at the gentlemen's clubs, but how much of it is really between genuine friends? And what about at the endless balls, parties, and outings of the ton—most of the conversations are about one-upmanship, showing off one's wealth, or just plain gossip. Has anyone ever had a proper conversation? Or does everyone wear a mask to try and put across the best version of themselves?*

Or even worse, the version of themselves their parents want the world to see? The version of themselves they've been trained to put on for Society's sake?

Now that Arthur was really thinking hard about it, he realized that the only type of conversations he usually overheard at such social events revolved around either artificial romance—in short, the marriage mart, getting noticed by the "right" people, or furthering one's business interests. No wonder he never let anyone in.

"Perhaps it is for the best," he muttered to himself, glad now to have found a private area in the garden where he could be alone, "that I do not have a friend to confide in."

Solitude could be his true calling. Maybe there were people in the world who were simply meant to be by themselves, and he was one of them. It was not the most pleasant sensation to feel, but if it was the truth then Arthur had no choice but to accept it. He had never truly fitted in with Polite Society, and that must be the reason why.

But what did that mean for Lady Greenfield? The poor, beautiful lady who was stuck in the middle of all of this, the person Edward Maxwell, Duke of York, had pushed into a corner and given very little time to make such an important decision.

"What are you thinking now?" he wondered aloud as he pictured her. Her pale, heart-shaped face, those deliciously enchanting green eyes, her lovely red hair that cascaded down to the small of her back so fetchingly. "I am sorry if you are troubled."

The proposal had troubled her. It had been obvious to him from the look in her eyes. The way Miss Ellen had spoken was very eloquent, sincere too, but she did not seem to have mastered the art of hiding her feelings, as other ladies of his acquaintance did so skillfully, ensuring they always acted in a certain way in the presence of others. She did not hide her feelings well enough.

But Arthur loved the way that she talked. It hardly mattered that she did not sound exactly like the other grand ladies of the *ton*. He adored the natural way in which she spoke. He could listen to her talk all day long.

Maybe he would get the chance to listen to her talk much more as they got to know one another. If she agreed to that, of course. At this point, he had absolutely no idea what she was going to do, which was deeply troubling.

Did she like him? When they had locked eyes for a moment, it seemed she might, or could, given half the chance. But there was also the worry that she would see him as part of the problem. Part of the trap she might have to step into.

He did not like the way that felt. It was horrible.

Perhaps I should have spoken to her alone? Although being given such an opportunity would have been highly unlikely. Without a chaperone, which obviously would have had to have been his father since he must be in the middle of everything, he would not have been given the chance to talk to Miss Ellen. *But I could have explained. I could have let her know that this situation is none of my doing. I was as surprised as her at my father's offer of marriage. I only want what is best for her. I am not the money hungry man who wants to impress the King that my father is.*

Of course, she likely would not have believed him. She did not even know him. Miss Ellen did not look like the sort of woman who trusted people easily. She had a barrier in her eyes, a protectiveness, that was likely for her sisters as well as herself.

There was nothing Arthur could do. There was not a chance of talking to her privately, or of letting her know that, while his father's intentions were focused solely on enriching himself, he, Arthur, was the very opposite of that. It was hard to swallow, but he was going to have to accept that he would have no chance to make Miss Ellen see the truth.

She would have to think whatever she thought. He could not control it.

"My lord?" Suddenly, he was shaken from his deep thoughts by a voice. The butler stood nearby, clearly waiting for his attention. "Your father has been calling for you."

"Do you know why?" Arthur furrowed his brows in confusion. As far as he was aware, his father was far too busy today to even think about him.

"I believe he wants to talk to you about London, my lord."

"Oh. I see!" Arthur had almost forgotten that he was expected to travel to London very soon. "Of course, I shall go to him directly. Thank you."

The butler bowed and departed.

His father wanted him to go to London to take care of some business concerning the land he wanted to acquire. It was part of his father's attempts to school him in taking over the barley business. The only reason Arthur did not mind too much was that being in town would offer much needed distraction from his problems. He wanted something to help take his mind off the Greenfield sisters, Miss Ellen especially. Since there was nothing he could do to make her feel better or influence her decision, the best thing he could do was try to forget about it for now.

Although, that red hair, those green eyes, her stunning face—the memory would not be so easy to push aside, especially since the business did not interest him at all. He could only hope the journey and the bustle of town would distract him.

CHAPTER 8

THE CHANGE in the air seemed to come quickly as Arthur's carriage took him further away from the Maxwell estate. The thick clouds above were now darkening, so that they resembled ash.

The color reminded Arthur of the pallor of his father's face before he'd left the mansion. He truly did look sick, and the coughing fit the duke had suffered was unpleasant. But Arthur was still convinced the old man had sent him on this business trip because he wanted him to familiarize himself with the barley business—and the business of one day becoming the duke himself.

Rain threatened. It was sure to come soon. No doubt about it. Arthur could smell it in the air, but it was not quite ready to burst free from the clouds just yet. Arthur could only hope he would reach town before the skies opened.

Arthur whispered to himself. "This is the weather of uncertainty, and it always seems to come when I am uncertain about something."

Looking out of the carriage window and up at the sky, Arthur certainly felt that the weather had been sent specifically to match his mood.

Truth be told, Arthur was only thinking about the weather at all because he did not want to allow his mind to wander back to a certain subject. He knew that if he gave his thoughts any freedom at all, they would turn directly back to Miss Ellen. The countryside views along the way as they headed towards London were not providing the distraction he so desperately needed.

"I'm sure Miss Ellen would not like me thinking about her so much," he murmured to himself, glad to be alone with his thoughts. *She is in the midst of grief. Double grief. That is something I understand. I should not be so selfishly wondering what she is thinking about me.*

She really had seemed quite broken by the death of her father, as had her sisters. He must have been a wonderful man; his death had clearly been sudden and unexpected, cruelly snatching him away from his daughters much too quickly. Arthur wondered how different things would have been between them if he had met Miss Ellen her under normal circumstances. He wondered how well he would have gotten along with Mr. Greenfield. Clearly, they had a lot in common, since Ellen's father clearly had not been the type of man who put money before everything else, unlike his own father. The picture Miss Ellen had painted made him seem more like a family man.

Of course, Arthur was only making that assumption based on the little he knew about the Greenfield family, but he had nothing else to go on. Imagination, conjecture, assumptions—was all that was at his disposal. He had to use a large amount of guesswork to fill in the missing pieces of Miss Ellen's life and how different things might have been had their paths crossed in another way.... .

Although, if he really thought about it, without the tragedy that had taken over her life, his father would likely never have had reason to introduce him to Miss Ellen Greenfield. Without the proposed financial benefits promised by the acquisition of the Greenfield estate, his father never would have considered someone like her as a wife for his son. He would have put status and the size of a potential wife's dowry over and above Arthur's wants and needs. In normal circumstances, he and Miss Ellen would likely never have even met.

Perhaps marrying me might not be such a bad thing for her and her sisters. I certainly hope she sees it that way. But if she feels forced to by the dire financial situation is dire—well, that may be, I will show her I am a good man, and I will do what I can to make her happy.

He was a better man than his father; he knew it. He shuddered at the thought of Miss Ellen being stuck with a money-hungry man like the duke. She was far too wonderful for that. Judging from the short time he had spent with her, she seemed lovely. Kind-hearted, sweet-natured, sensible . . . and caring when it came to her family.

Oh dear, I'm not doing a very good job of not thinking about Miss Ellen, am I? She's been on my mind the entire time. He gave himself a mental shake, reminding himself that it would be a good idea to think instead about the business ahead. His father had entrusted him with the task, had given him this responsibility, even if it was a small one. To be sure, Arthur knew the assignment was intended to drag him into his father's business dealings when he did not want that path for himself. But that did not mean he was not going to give it his all.

In a way, he reflected, he was a little like his father, in the sense that he always gave his responsibilities his full commitment and saw them through diigently. At least that was one positive thing to have come out of his upbringing. He might not have inherited all his father's traits, but he did have that one.

~

By the time Arthur reached the client's office in London, the rain was falling hard and heavy, as if the Lord himself were crying. The sky had well and truly opened, the gray clouds were now black and angry. The gloom made Arthur feel rather somber.

All he wanted to do was get in and out of his business meeting as quickly as possible so he could get back home. Nothing beneficial that he'd hoped to gain from the trip to London had come about. He was still caught up in his emotions, feeling deeply upset about things he could not control.

Everything related to Miss Ellen continued to plague him. That was not going to change. In the end, Arthur was going to have to find some kind of solution—or it would end up driving him insane.

The carriage came to a halt outside the trader's office, and he descended onto street, stretching his legs and anticipating the business meeting with some trepidation. He regretted his unsettled, troubled mood. But it did not matter that he was not feeling ready for the meeting; it was happening.

Arthur sucked in a slightly shaky breath before rolling his shoulders back and jutting out his chin, trying to project an air of confidence.

If he could not feel confidence, he would pretend he did he had it. It was the sort of mask that he did not mind wearing because it was useful.

"Thank you kindly," Arthur said to the coachman with a nod. "Wait here if you please. I hope I shall not be too long."

The coachman nodded in response. Arthur would not have minded staying there, standing in the busy street next to the carriage, rather than dealing with the trader. But he had no choice. His father had given his instructions, which must be obeyed.

"Ah, my dear marquess." The trader lit up the moment he spotted Arthur. "Your father sent word you would be coming. How pleasant it is to see you. I have always admired the way that your father does business, so I am looking forward to working with you as well."

A coldness settled over Arthur. There was something about the situation he did not like. Anyone who respected the way the duke did business did not sit right with him.

He also thought it best not to bring up his father's poor health, just in case.

"How do you do, sir? Pleased to make your acquaintance too."

He bowed, shook the man's hand, and tried to smile, but Arthur could not quite manage it. He simply did not want to be here. His father should have been the one to deal with this.

"I must tell you, I have heard whispers that your father might be doing dealings with the King," the trader said with a grin. "Why, you must be extremely happy about that. I cannot even imagine."

Arthur could not deal with that at all. It was yet another annoying reminder that everyone saw him as identical in nature to his father.

"I really couldn't say. Shall we stick to business? If you don't mind, of course," he said with a thin smile. "I'm sure your time is precious."

The trader looked a little taken aback. Clearly, he had been expecting a cozy chat before getting down to business, but Arthur was not prepared for that. He simply wanted to get what he had to do finished so he could get back home as soon as possible.

Thankfully, the trader agreed, and they took their seats to talk, covering only what needed to be discussed.

"So, your father has entrusted you with this business?" The trader smirked at Arthur as he spoke, irritating him again. "That is a rather big step."

"You think so?" Arthur found himself snapping. "I am his son and heir. Why should he not trust me?" Arthur did not really know why he was allowing himself to be provoked by the man, whom he did not know at all, just because he had made some assumptions about him. Arthur did not even want this responsibility; he was not interested in his father's work at all. But he did not enjoy being looked down upon in such a condescending manner, especially not when the trader's comments implied a questioning of his abilities. Perhaps that defensiveness was another thing he had inherited from his father.

"Of course, my lord." The trader held up his hands in surrender. "I meant no offense. Of course, you are you are your fathers trusted agent, no doubt about that."

Arthur shifted awkwardly in his seat. "My father wishes for your advice when it comes to his military commissions. Should he continue with the current commissions or is it time for him to work up the ranks?"

"Well, as I have said to your father in the past, the higher the rank, the more costly things become and the higher the responsibility. If one wishes to purchase commissions of officers, one must remember that they are on the front lines, risking their lives for the country."

"So, then. The greater the rewards, in that case." Arthur said, desperate to show the trader he understood how the system worked.

"That is correct. Although, I assume you have been sent with instructions? I do not think the duke would send you all the way here merely for advice."

It was a test, and Arthur knew it. Not just a test from this man, but from his father as well. The duke wanted to know if his son had it in him to take risks when it came to business—but the right risks. The Duke of York wanted to see that he had raised an astute son who could take over the business, even if he had made it clear that he did not wish to. Perhaps Arthur should take this chance to prove to his father that he was not to be trusted. That he was not interested and never would be. But at the same time, he felt the trader judging him, and he wanted to show the man he was capable. Just because he did not want something, did not mean he wished to be seen as incompetent. "I think we should discuss some higher ranks," he said with a challenging smile to the trader. "I am sure that is what my father intends."

The trader nodded with satisfaction. Arthur had risen to the challenge, and he was about to put his father's business at risk. Hopefully, it would be a risk that paid off in the end.

～

Exhaustion threatened to consume Arthur as he slumped back into his carriage seat. The meeting had been a nightmare. Arthur knew he had done a very good job, that his father was going to be very proud of him when he got back home.

But that did not make Arthur any keener to get back there. He did not want to face his father just yet. In fact, the meeting with the trader, and the way he had made Arthur feel, only made him even more determined to try and achieve the impossible.

Since he was in town, his business concluded, and he was free for the time being, the idea had been growing in his mind to take a short detour on the way home. Might he pay a call at the Greenfield home? Not to put pressure on Miss Ellen to make a decision, but simply to have the chance to try and set the record straight, to conquer the unpleasant feeling that had settled in his stomach as he waited for her answer.

The answer he had become increasingly desperate to hear. Ever since first meeting the oldest Greenfield daughter, a spark had ignited within him, and it could not be doused. It was more than just wanting her to know that he was not like his father; there was a magnetic pull that he felt was drawing them together. Arthur was not sure why that should be the case, but he knew it was unlike any connection he had ever felt before. The fact that it was inexplicable intrigued him more.

He felt absolutely compelled to let Miss Ellen know that he had the sisters' best interests at heart, without the duke hovering over him. He hoped that by visiting the Greenfield home, he would be able to make the girls see that he himself did not want to put any pressure on them and that he was a good person. If Miss Ellen decided that marriage to him was the best way forward for her family, he wanted to assure her that he would be a good husband to her.

It might not be the ideal way she had planned to meet her future husband, but Arthur was sure he could make her happy, given half the chance.

Arthur did not know if it was a good idea to call on her. He knew his father would be absolutely furious if he found out, but that did not stop him from leaning forward to give the change of destination to his coach driver.

If he did not take the chance to do it now, then he would always regret it. Whatever way things turned out, he would know that he'd tried his best —even if he failed in the end.

CHAPTER 9

THINGS WERE NOT GOING to plan. Ellen darted her eyes back and forth between her sisters as the exchange grew louder by the moment. Thank goodness the Greenfield family no longer had many servants to worry about, because having them overhear the argument that was raging between the sisters in the middle of the drawing room would be incredibly embarrassing.

As the oldest sister, Ellen would have to try and step in the middle of it to calm things down before it really got out of hand. Luckily, for now, she could sit back and let things happen, because at that moment, she did not have the energy to do anything.

"I cannot believe you, Gracelyn!" Joy yelled, red rage burning her cheeks as she stood nose to nose with her sister. "You are being so selfish. You cannot force Ellen to do something she does not want to, especially not get married to a complete stranger simply because you are worried about money! Ellen has the right to refuse. You know as well as I do, she wants to marry for love!"

Ellen swallowed hard. She had hoped this "meeting" would be much more constructive than it was proving to be. She could hardly comprehend the anger crackling in the air between her sisters. They appeared to feel the emotional pressure of the situation even more than herself!

Perhaps, with all her worrying and sorrow, she had simply become numb to it all.

"Joy, I am not being selfish," Gracelyn yelled back. "Do not say that!"

"You are!" Joy threw up her hands in frustration. "Your selfish behavior is becoming increasingly unbearable as the days go on. I cannot under-stand you."

"Unbearable," Gracelyn snorted in a very unladylike manner. "I am the only one here who is capable of being realistic, it seems. This is not a fairy tale situation. We are not talking about some romantic "happily ever after" here." The defiant, burning words came flying out of Gracelyn's mouth. The row was escalating, and Ellen felt too stunned to stop it. "We need this. Ellen has to marry the Marquess. What other choices do we have, Joy? Please tell me."

"I do not know," Joy admitted, but without the anger in her tone dissi-pating. "I do not have all the answers, I admit that. But I believe that, together, we can come up with a better solution. But we must work together to find it. It is what Father would want."

Joy's words echoed Ellen's own when the discussion had begun, but, of course, Gracelyn had completely ignored them, just as she continued to do now. Ellen could see how angry she was by the way her fists curled up and her eyes flashed.

"Be realistic, Joy. Think about what else we can do. We have no money for a dowry anymore, nor do we have a male family member to introduce us to gentlemen. And take a look out of the window, Joy. See what has become of our land. I know it used to be beautiful and green and productive, but it is not anymore. And without money to improve the land, what can we do? The duke is offering us a lifeline—and you wish to reject it!"

Joy tried to calm herself and walked slowly towards the window. She might not have liked what Gracelyn had said, but she forced herself to look at what lay outside. Ellen held her breath as she waited to see what Joy would say next.

Ellen already knew what Gracelyn thought, so Joy's final opinion would be vitally important in the decision Ellen had to make. If the youngest sister could think of any other way out of the horrible situation, then Ellen wanted to hear it.

"I do not like this at all." Joy folded her arms across her chest and shook her head. Ellen could not see her facial expression, but she could imagine it. Joy was not impressed one bit. Her eyebrows were likely furrowed, and her nose screwed up. "I do not like this one bit, but . . . I am not sure what other option there is."

"I told you!" Gracelyn snapped, celebrating being right, clearly not thinking about Ellen's feelings at all. "That is why I say what I say! Because I know there is no other way that we can survive."

Gracelyn caught Ellen's eyes. Her expression suddenly softened and she dropped her head for a moment.

"We do not have anyone anymore," Gracelyn continued in a calmer tone of voice. "Without Father, we do not have anyone else to rely on anymore. We only have one another. This might not be an ideal situation for anyone, but I cannot see any other way out. I am glad you can see it now, Sister. This marriage will be for best." Gracelyn stated, then she shrugged her shoulders. "If I'd had the offer, I would leap at it. But the marquess does not want me."

Ellen breathed deeply before she rose to her feet and joined Joy at the window. Joy stared at her with wide eyes and backed away, leaving Ellen alone to take in the view.

Much as she wanted to cling to the past and their father's dreams for the estate, Gracelyn was right; the happy, prosperous times were not coming back. Without any money to put into the land, it was never going to be productive. The fields full of crops, the livestock were all gone. Without productive land and the income it created, the estate was all but worthless to them. There were no good marriage prospects for any of the sisters. Things could only descend into a vicious cycle . . . until there was nothing left at all.

Gracelyn was right: the duke's offer was a lifeline. And even if Ellen did not want to, she was going to have to grasp it with both hands. In truth, the meeting with her sisters had only confirmed what she already knew. She was going to have to prepare for a wedding.

The drenched, empty landscape beyond the window only confirmed it. Only money could bring the land back to life. Nothing would improve on the estate without major investment, investment the Greenfield girls lacked the means to make.

As much as she'd wanted to avoid it, the decision was already made.

Ellen blinked back tears. She hated the sense of letting her father down, giving away all his hard work, the idea that, by agreeing to this marriage, she would be erasing his memory completely.

It was the last thing she had ever wanted to do.

Gracelyn seemed to think there were other ways to hang on to their father's memory, and Ellen was going to have to hope she was right.

"Very well," she finally said as she spun around to face her sisters. "I suppose it is time for me to get to know the Marquess of York a little better, then."

"To see if you *will* marry him?" Gracelyn gasped in pleased surprise.

"Well, much as I am staunchly opposed to a loveless marriage, I do not see that I have any other choice in the matter. I shall spend time with the man because I must."

Everyone was silent for a moment, and Joy and Gracelyn exchanged a look. Ellen thought she must not have been clear enough in her response.

"So, you will agree to the duke's offer?"

Ellen understood her sister's question; it was not merely her selfish outlook speaking. As much as she might not like it, Gracelyn was simply looking after herself, and Joy as well. If anything, Ellen told herself, she was the one who had been selfish by putting them all through this agonizing time of indecision.

"I will let the duke know that my decision has been made," Ellen confirmed. "Thank you both so much for talking this through with me, I appreciate your help. I know this has not been the easiest discussion, but I am grateful for your opinions."

She could hear Joy and Gracelyn whispering as she walked out the room, but Ellen chose not to worry about what they were saying. She was doing what they thought best, so they could not be critical of her.

Perhaps they were excitedly planning the wedding already, thinking of everything Ellen would rather ignore. For now, she was simply going to concentrate on getting to know the marquess— so they would have at least some small foundation to build their marriage upon.

She could not imagine liking the man ever, let alone loving him. They would never share the same views or moral outlook, since he was clearly a man of business, like his father. But that was not something she had a choice in anymore. Ellen was simply going to have to become one of those people trapped in a marriage that was more of a prison than a pleasure. The fate she had so strongly rejected for her life was now going to be exactly what she must face.

There were many women who had faced similar fates, she knew it. Ellen would probably meet other wives in the same position as her once she was let into the secret world of married folk. Being married to a marquess was certainly going to open many social doors for her; she would get to know the *ton;* she might even leave the person she was now far behind. High society might change her completely.

No, I cannot let that happen. Father will forgive a lot of things; he will understand why we've had to make this decision, but if I lose myself, he will never be happy.

The importance of being herself was something her father had always tried to impress upon her, and her sisters as well, which was why their personalities clashed at times and there were fallouts among them.

But this time, there had not really been any fall-out because, even throughout all the shouting, the girls had ended up on the same side. Even if they had come from other sides of the spectrum, there was one thing they all agreed on.

Ellen had no choice but to marry Arthur Maxwell, Marquess of York.

That was the end of it.

CHAPTER 10

THE RAIN HAD NOT SLOWED DOWN by the time night fell over the English countryside. Ellen was alone in her bed, her eyes drifting around her bed chamber as she acknowledged every trinket, every detail, every little thing that characterized the space as her own. Her heart broke with every new thing she saw. The ornaments she adored, the beautiful dressing table that had once belonged to her mother, the lamp which shone out in different colors, always cheering her up. . . .

Soon enough, it would all be gone. Faster than she knew it, she would no longer have a space to call her own, a place she could decorate just the way she wanted to. Her space would be shared with a man she barely knew, a man she was going to have to live with, sleep with, for the rest of her life, whether she liked it or not.

Everything in her present life was going to end, and a new life was about to begin. She would not be allowed to be herself. She would have to fit in with this man's expectations, a man who seemed hungry for land and money. She would have to learn to be the perfect lady he wanted on his arm whenever it suited him. But without love, marriage would be absolutely horrible.

Unless . . . oh, God, was she really thinking about it? Was she really considering doing something to ruin things before it even got off the ground? Because she really did not want to marry the man if she could help it. But she was going to have to if he wished it.

But if the Marquess of York choses to reject me, then what can I do about it?

Perhaps it was a "middle of the night" thought. One that came to her because she had not had enough sleep. But it was all too tempting. Because if the marquess turned her down as a prospective wife as they were getting acquainted, then she could not be blamed for anything that followed. Her sisters could not be angry at her. Instead, they might focus on finding another solution to their financial problems.

Ellen could not help but find herself increasingly attracted to the idea. So much so, that she climbed out of her bed and began to pace the room quickly. What if this was some subliminal message from her father letting her know that she was not supposed to marry this man after all? Much as she thought she had been backed into a corner, perhaps that wasn't the case after all? Ellen wanted there to be another solution. Anything else but *this*!

"What do I do, Papa?" Ellen whispered into the universe, desperately begging her father to give her an answer. "If I do not marry the marquess and allow the duke to take over the lands you have worked so hard for, then what should I do? I would love to have you here telling me exactly what to do. I am not yet ready to make all of these life-changing decisions all by myself."

If she had to marry that man for the sake of her sisters, then she would, but if there was any other way, then she wanted to take it. Anything at all.

Ellen felt herself turn towards her bookcase. The bright, white moonlight streamed in through the window and illuminated her favorite books. Whether it was a message from her father, Ellen was not sure. But in the middle of the night, she chose to take it as a cue. There *was* something else she could do.

Ellen practically tiptoed over to the bookcase and ran her fingers over some of the spines, waiting for one to jump out at her. As she did so, she caught an accidental glimpse of herself in the mirror which took her aback.

She was not looking very appealing just then. If only the marquess could see her at that moment, with her hair sticking up all over the place and her face flooded with the tiredness she could not disguise. He would run for the hills!

"Oh, is that what I should do, Father?" She ran her fingers down her soft cheeks, not taking her eyes off the fright she appeared in the mirror. "Make myself as unappealing as possible to the marquess so that he runs away?"

She might not be able to do it with her looks because Gracelyn would immediately notice what she was doing. She would be utterly furious about it. Ellen deliberately ruining their chances of a financial rescue would be sacrilegious for her. She had only just gotten Ellen to agree to the marriage, and she was bound to be on edge until wedding was over.

Plus, Marquess of York seemed far too intelligent to fall for that ruse. He had already seen her, so wearing her hair in an unflattering style or dressing in unattractive clothing would do no good. Instead, she was going to have to utilize the qualities he did not already know.

It will have to be my personality. That is what he knows little of—and what he will want to learn about as we spend time together.

But what could she actually do in that respect? Again, plain rudeness would not go down well; it would have to be something a lot more subtle than that, but something guaranteed to put off the marquess before any wedding could take place. Once the vows were spoken, it would be too late.

Ellen took a step back, stumbling into the bookshelf because of the darkness shrouding her and the exhaustion flooding her brain. As she bumped her head, a memory suddenly flooded back to her, like a vision placed in her brain.

It was the summertime, a hot, humid day, and all the young girls were enjoying the sun, loving the time away from their parents to play outside the Greenfield estate. All except for Ellen. Ellen wanted to read some of her fairy tale romance novels.

"Come and play!" the neighbor girl called to her. *"You're mad! Only mad people would choose to read when they could be having fun. Why won't you come and run around with us? Mad! Mad! Mad, that's what you are, Ellen Greenfield!"*

Mad . . . it had been meant as an insult at the time, one that stung too. She'd actually raced back inside the house, leaving behind her favorite reading spot underneath the willow tree. She might have spent too much of the summer in her bedroom, hiding away with her books, avoiding the outside world, but her father always told her to simply be herself. . . .

A little smile spread across her face. What if she was "herself" in front of Arthur? Not the proper lady destined to be a duchess one day but the crazy girl who was teased all summer long. It could not simply be for reading all the time, as it had been back then, because that might not be noticed. But what if she really did seem mad? The sort of madness to make a man fearful of being in her presence for any period of time.

"I could pull that off, I'm sure," she muttered to herself in a little voice. "I could act mad and hide it from everyone else but him. I could make it so Arthur would rather walk barefoot through the snow before marrying me."

Ellen picked up a couple of the books, wondering if any of her favorite main characters had done something similar. No, that was unlikely, since the stories she preferred always had a "happily ever after". But perhaps there was a character on whom she could model her new, crazy personality on. It was an idea definitely worth researching.

"Oh, if only things were different," she murmured to herself. "This scheme would be something Gracelyn would adore. She would be utterly brilliant at it too."

A lump formed in Ellen's throat as the realization hit her that even if her plan worked, it might not be the end of the marquess' presence in her life. Because Gracelyn had already expressed a determination to marry the man in a heartbeat should he ask her. Whether that was because she saw something in him or simply to help the family out, it hardly mattered. The result would still be something very strange.

But only to me. Not to society. So . . . I shall just have to just get on with it by myself.

Unfortunately, she would not be able to tell Joy either, so she could not ask for advice about her plan. Joy was the person she was closest to in the whole world, someone she knew she could trust, but she could not put it past Gracelyn's ability to get the truth out of her little sister. If the middle sister caught on to a secret, she would be relentless and make Joy's life a living hell until she gave in and told her everything.

The wedge that would drive between the sisters would be unbearable. Since they were all they had in the whole world, that could not happen. It was unthinkable.

No, as much as it was going to isolate her and make her even lonelier than she was just then, if this was the plan she decided upon, then she would have to execute it completely by herself, with no help from anyone.

Except, maybe from her father, if he really was watching over her and looking out for her, which Ellen had become confident he must be after the events of the night.

Eventually, Ellen took herself to bed, this time feeling a lot more

relaxed and actually able to close her eyes. Just knowing she was not actually trapped in a corner as she had thought helped a lot. The anxiety that
had been careering through her body ever since the family meeting and
the awful argument dissipated just a little.

If that was not a sign that her plan was sound, then Ellen had no idea
what was. It *must* be her father communicating with her, just as she had
asked him to, so it was only right to follow his advice.

If feigning madness for a little while ensured she could keep her
father's home and land while also protecting her sisters, then that was all
she wanted. After this debacle was all over, then the Greenfield sisters
could come together to work out another plan. One that would suit them
all and keep them all happy.

Ellen could not wait until that moment. It would be such a weight off
her shoulders.

CHAPTER 11

ARTHUR WAS a day later reaching the Greenfield house than he'd first planned, delayed by the troubles caused by the rain. It was far too dangerous to travel, so Arthur had been forced to find accommodation for a night. But now he was here, and excited.

He knocked on the door, shifting his feet awkwardly as he waited for someone to answer. That was a big difference between the Greenfield home and his own; at the Maxwell mansion, the door would have been answered right away. But, of course, the Maxwell estate had an army of servants to attend to the family's every whim. The Greenfield ladies were severely lacking in that department.

"Oh!" The door swung open, and Arthur was surprised to see Miss Gracelyn standing before him. The middle Greenfield sister had a lot of similarities to Miss Ellen but much more fire in her eyes. She seemed to have a lot of anger held in her heart, which Arthur did not know the source of.

"Good morning, Marquess. . . " she said, clearly recovering from her shock at seeing him.

"Indeed, it is, Miss Gracelyn. I hope you ladies will not think me rude for calling so unexpectedly." He doffed his hat and bowed politely. "As you can see, my father is not with me. I have come, as there are some matters I would prefer to discuss with your family without his presence."

"So . . . the duke does not know you are here?" Miss Gracelyn asked, eyes wide.

"He does not. And I would prefer that it stays that way."

Miss Gracelyn nodded slowly, accepting the disclaimer easily. "Please, my lord, do come inside. Let me take your hat and coat. Perhaps you would like to wait in the parlor for a few moments? I shall call my sisters at once."

The parlor was not a grand room. Perhaps it had been once upon a time but not anymore, with its old-fashioned, somewhat shabby furniture and outdated decor. Still, it had a pleasing sense of family ease and warmth about it that his own home lacked. Unfortunately, it was also a rather unwelcome reminder to Arthur that money really did make a big difference to people's lives. He had always lived in such luxury that he took it for granted, so seeing the shabby state of the Greenfield home opened his eyes somewhat.

"Marquess." Arthur was jolted from his thoughts by the musical lilt of Miss Ellen's voice. It was a voice he had been thinking about ever since first meeting her. "Good morning, my lord, this is unexpected," she added, coming into the room.

Arthur bowed and Miss Ellen curtsied right back. Miss Gracelyn and Miss Joy followed behind their older sister, both curtseying demurely and eyeing him with great interest.

"I do apologize for this unexpected visit, ladies. But there are some things I would like to discuss with you without my father present, if that is convenient, of course." He finished, sucking in a slightly shaky breath. Just because he had been planning this speech for a very long time, throughout the whole journey home, in fact, did not mean he was ready to actually deliver it in front of three pairs of inquisitive green eyes.

"During my last visit—with my father—I feel as if my father—well, that he might have given you the wrong impression of myself and my family. " He paused to compose himself before continuing, "I wished to have the opportunity to correct any misapprehensions on that account."

"I do not understand quite what you mean, my lord. You are concerned that we may think badly of you for some reason? Please, do sit down, won't you?" Miss Ellen gestured to a sofa, and Arthur sat down, cleating his throat, feeling awkward. She folded her hands in her lap as she took a seat on the sofa opposite and was immediately flanked by her sisters.

"I, er, suppose so, yes," he said, feeling his cheeks redden.

"Then there is absolutely nothing for you to worry about, I assure you, " Miss Ellen said with a gracious nod. She glanced at her siters, who also nodded in agreement, both agog, as if they had a front seat at the opera.

"In fact, since you are here, it seems like the ideal time for me to tell you that I have decided to accept your father's proposal. Having had the opportunity to think it over, as your father so generously allowed, I *do* think a match between us would be a very good idea." She smiled dazzlingly at him. The sisters smiled and nodded.

"Oh!" Arthur was a little taken aback by her sudden announcement, recalling the panic in her eyes when the marriage was first mooted. Her outright acceptance was not what he'd expected at all.

He swallowed hard and tried to smile. "Ah. I see. Well, that is very good news. I am pleased." He gazed at her, entranced, for a moment, as the cogs ticked around in his brain.

"Yes, my lord, is there something more you wish to say?" she asked sweetly, disconcertingly. Much as Arthur had wished for this acceptance, there was one question he wanted answered before going further.

"May I—may I ask what made you decide to accept me?"

Miss Ellen's eyes widened. The question had evidently taken her by surprise. "Oh. Well. . ."

Miss Gracelyn nudged her in the side. She might have thought the action was discrete, but Arthur spotted it and tried his hardest to suppress a smile as Miss Ellen shot her sister a warning look.

"I suppose . . . one could say . . . I was thinking like a child before, being rather sentimental, I suppose. And I was so utterly surprised, the offer being so unexpected, you understand?" Miss Ellen explained. "But now I am thinking like a lady, a lady with responsibilities to her family."

Arthur liked her answer. It satisfied him because it laid all his worries to rest. The delay in acceptance had nothing to do with him but was instead due to her own concerns . . . and the element of surprise, of course.

"Of course. Your . . . hesitation was perfectly understandable in the circumstances . . . having just lost your father, I mean. And the surprise, too."

He inwardly sighed with relief. Perhaps everything was going to be all right after all.

Arthur was just about to peak again, but before he could get a word out, Miss Ellen rose unexpectedly to her feet and went to the windows. It did not seem the usual thing to do in the middle of a conversation, so Arthur was dumbstruck. As he caught the eyes of the other Greenfield sisters, he realized they were puzzled too by their sister's actions. What on earth was going on?

Miss Ellen drew back the curtain and examined the rain outside for a few moments. There was a strange tension in the air which Arthur could not fathom the reason for. His eyes darted between all three sisters, but he did not find an explanation for Miss Ellen's odd behavior in any of their expressions. Neither Miss Gracelyn nor Miss Joy seemed to know what was going on. It was very strange.

"Oh, my goodness!" Miss Ellen suddenly cried out, clapping her hands together in childish glee. "It is strange, is it not? That the raindrops are so *nosy*. Just like the birds and rabbits. It seems that my sisters can never have any privacy."

What? Arthur's eyebrows shot up into his hairline. *What did she mean?* Miss Ellen hardly sounded like herself at all, and certainly nothing like the lovely woman he'd spoken to when his father was in the room.

Perhaps she had been wearing her mask then, and now, without the duke here, she was showing her true personality.

Finally, just to break the strangeness of the moment, Lady Gracelyn let out a nervous chuckle. "I am terribly sorry, marquess, I do not understand my sister's newfound sense of humor either. She must believe she is very funny."

Arthur nodded at her slowly. He was almost too anxious to turn back to Miss Ellen once more just to see her expression.

"It is quite alright, my lady," Arthur finally replied, forcing his lips to smile. "I understand that your family has been under quite a lot of strain lately."

While Miss Gracelyn was focusing her attention entirely on him, as if to distract him, Miss Joy was still staring confusedly over at her sister by the window. As nervous as the situation was making him feel, he nevertheless twisted around in his seat to see Miss Ellen staring blankly out at the raindrops once more and scratching her head as if she thought she had spiders crawling through that beautiful red hair of hers.

This was not the lady whom he had been thinking about ever constantly since leaving the Greenfield home only a short time before. *This* lady was making him feel uneasy. The excitement he felt earlier about marrying her had sunk uncomfortably to the pit of his stomach.

Was he making her feel uncomfortable? Was that why she was acting so strangely? Because she had seemed so different, so charming the other day.

Arthur decided it was time for him to leave. He must excuse himself and get out of the house before the situation grew even more odd. But he did not wish to be rude. He had to concoct a plausible excuse—and quickly.

"Well, I believe—"

He was cut off as a loud banging sound coming from the front door ricocheted through the house, startling Arthur and the two ladies sitting opposite him. If this was yet another visitor to the Greenfield home, it might be his excuse to leave. No one would think him rude then. Indeed, it would be the right thing to do.

"Please, Joy, answer the door, would you?" Miss Gracelyn said to her younger sister, suspicion in her eyes, as if she did not wish to leave Miss Ellen alone.

Miss Joy jumped up and practically ran from the room. The whole visit had become very strange and uncomfortable, and he almost wished he had not come at all. He shifted awkwardly in his seat, wishing he could simply take off and run from the house.

Miss Ellen was still scratching her head furiously over by the window, and Miss Gracelyn was staring at him so hard that he feared her eyes might pierce him. It was awful.

"Is he here?" bellowed a familiar voice.

Arthur's spine stiffened. He would recognize that booming voice anywhere, and terror shot through him. It was his father! But how? And he did not sound happy at all. There was rage in his tone, which only added to the terror that gripped Arthur.

Now, any feelings he had about the Greenfield sisters no longer mattered. His father's anger was far more frightening to him than anything else in the world.

"He is here, I know my son is here. I have already seen his carriage outside. But what is he doing here? You cannot hide him from me!" the duke boomed, his boots stamping more loudly toward the parlor with every moment.

Arthur rose to his feet, ready to accept whatever was about to come his way. He couldn't deny his presence; he had been caught out. Although, that acceptance did not stop his heart from pounding like a hammer against his rib cage. He fought to catch his breath. His brain spun wildly as he struggled to come up with a good explanation for being in the Greenfield parlor, something, anything to try to calm his father down. But as previous experience told him, that was impossible. Once his father's ire was up, that was it. Until he got it out of his system himself, there was nothing anyone could do.

"You have come here behind my back," the Duke York growled as he stormed into the parlor and spotted Arthur transfixed on the settee. "I cannot believe what you have done! What are you plotting, boy? You are supposed to be doing business in London! I am shocked! I am speechless at your perfidy!"

Well, he's hardly speechless, Arthur thought helplessly, but that was beside the point.

Arthur opened and closed his mouth a couple of times like a fish and stared at his father's red face. He did not know how to respond. His intentions in coming here had been noble in his eyes, and to suggest he was plotting against his father was ridiculous, of course. But he had come to see the sisters behind his father's back.

There was no denying that fact.

CHAPTER 12

ARTHUR FLOUNDERED in the face of his father's rage. He wanted so badly to defend himself, but his father's expression deeply unnerved him. He had never seen him looking as inflamed with passion as he did at that moment. Arthur had pushed him too far.

"Are you going to explain to me what you're doing here?" The duke glared at his son, flames of fury flickering in his gaze. He completely ignored the terrified women. "Because I do not understand it."

"I am here—" Arthur started slowly, "because I wish to get better acquainted with Miss Ellen Greenfield. We did not have the opportunity to speak together previously."

"What are you talking about?" Edward flung his arms in the air in irritation. "You came with me, your father! Things were done in the proper manner. Miss Ellen spoke to you while I was here, chaperoning you. Why should you need to come here alone?"

How could Arthur explain that he wished to distinguish himself from his ruthless father without enraging the old man further? He was going to have to choose his words very carefully so the situation did not deteriorate even more.

"Miss Ellen was . . . unsure about the, er, proposal," he said carefully, hoping he was not upsetting the lady by saying that, considering she had already been behaving strangely. "So . . . I wanted to give her more of a chance to get to know me. That is what we agreed on, Father, was it not? That we two should spend some time together to make the decision easier for Miss Ellen." He was going to have to remind the duke what was at stake here. If he could make his father think of the King, things would doubtless improve at once. "To ensure the lady is happy with me and accepts the . . proposal."

The duke's face flickered with annoyance. Arthur had no idea what his father's next outburst might be, and he could hardly keep himself composed. Nerves zigzagged through his body. He was sure he was about to go mad too.

"That does not excuse your behavior." The duke's tone calmed a little. "I am not happy with you at all, Arthur. You cannot meet your . . . intended . . . without a chaperone, whatever your reasoning is. It is not how people behave."

"But Miss Ellen's sisters are here, and I am an adult." Arthur knew he probably should not have said that last bit because he risked sparking the flames of anger once more. But he had to push his point, to make sure everything was out in the open. "I should be permitted to have conversations with other adults without being chaperoned."

"I wonder sometimes if you understand anything about the way things work."

"Well, Miss Ellen has agreed to marry me, so I think it has all worked out splendidly, don't you, Father?"

Edward turned his eyes to stare at Miss Ellen, who stood frozen by the window like deer caught breaking cover by a hungry wolf. Panic crossed her face. "I should still like us to become better acquainted, my lord," she said, her words almost tripping over one another in haste.

The duke rolled his eyes in clear irritation. Arthur could see the distrust in the old man's look. If it was not for the Greenfield land the duke so desperately needed, he would have put an end to the situation already.

"You do remember, Miss Ellen, that time is of the essence here? You do not have all the time in the world to make this decision. A few days, that is all."

"Yes," Miss Gracelyn jumped in, speaking on her sister's behalf. "Yes, we understand the terms, Your Grace. We are truly sorry for the delay."

The duke did not even glance at her. He wanted assurances from the horse's mouth. But Miss Ellen said nothing. Her eyes seemed to be scanning the room frantically, as if she could hear a voice no one else could. It was worrying to watch her because there was definitely something happening to her that no one else could see. What did it mean? What was happening inside her mind?

"Very well," the duke declared with resignation. Clearly, he could see he was not going to get an answer from Miss Ellen. Or certainly not one he wished to hear, anyway. "I think it is time for us to leave. My son will not be calling alone again, I can assure you. Ladies." He nodded brusquely at the women.

There was a warning in his father's tone. He was not going to let Arthur out of his sight, no matter what happened. Arthur was not going to be given the chance to prove himself to Miss Ellen, to make her see that he was really nothing like his father. He could only hope that this debacle alone would be enough to convince her of that.

Arthur darted his eyes back towards Ellen, hoping to communicate with her silently, but she was still searching the room frantically with her eyes, as though a demon had crawled into her brain and was slowly taking over her body and mind.

It was strange, and more than a little unsettling. Goose bumps popped up all over his arms. He hardly wanted to take his eyes off her because he needed to reassure her that everything really was going to be fine, even if she did not that reassurance. But she was not looking at him. He might as well have not been there at all. She barely even acknowledged the chaos surrounding her.

Edward grabbed on to Arthur's arm and yanked him from the house. He pulled his son into his own carriage so that he could not travel home alone. That was how Arthur knew he was really in for it. He was in so much trouble. His life was going to be quite unpleasant for a very long time. . . .

～

Later that night, over dinner, Arthur relished the silence for a little while. His father had been shouting his opinions about Arthur's actions all day long, so it was nice to have a moment free from yelling.

But Arthur also had an idea floating around in his brain, and this was the first chance he'd had since their return home to suggest it: To tell his father that he knew just what he wanted to do to try and speed things up with Miss Ellen.

"Father, it would be a good idea if we threw a ball."

"Throw a ball?" Edward snapped. "Now, why should we do that?"

He was a man who tolerated social events if it helped him with his business, but he did not enjoy them. He certainly was not a man to put his hard-earned money into a holding a social event if it was not going to benefit him financially. But that did not stop Arthur.

"To celebrate my engagement to Miss Ellen Greenfield."

His heart was pounding in his with nerves. Was he anxious because he awaited his father's response to the suggestion with trepidation? Or because of Miss Ellen? Miss Ellen and her strangeness behavior today? He had been thinking a lot about it and had eventually landed on the following explanation: Miss Ellen had behaved so strangely because he had broken protocol by calling on her without a chaperone. Without her own father there and his father absent too, had he risked her reputation? No wonder she was upset with him.

But he was going to make it up to her, to make her see that he really was a good man who could make her happy given half the chance. The ball was just going to be a start of that. That was why he had to convince his father to go through with it because it was very important. The wedding might not happen without it.

"Your engagement?" The duke scraped back his chair and rose to his feet. "Oh, so it is an engagement now, is it? Because it certainly did not seem that way earlier today. In fact, Miss Ellen Greenfield does not look as if she wants to marry you at all."

A vice-like grip took hold of Arthur's lungs. He could hardly breathe, however hard he tried to suck in air. His father's suggestion did not sit right at all. Miss Ellen was the first woman who had made Arthur feel this way. He could not stand the idea of her not wanting him.

Maybe her behavior had been a little strange that afternoon, but that had not been enough to shut off his feelings. He understood it was her grief affecting her, and her concern for her reputation.

"I think she is just trying to be careful," Arthur replied in a rasping tone of voice. "I think she would simply like to get to know me a little before we are married. That is not unreasonable. But she did agree to the proposal before you arrived, so I am confident in her answer."

"You trust this woman?" The duke sneered, as if to suggest that no woman could ever be trusted. It was not the first time Arthur had been exposed to that sort of opinion from his father, and it disgusted him. He himself had never felt that way. "I think you are very naive. I think you are acting foolishly," the duke added scathingly.

"That might be true, but when she agrees, we are going to have to have a ball, so I do not see why we should put off the inevitable."

Arthur knew he was pushing his father a little too far, but this was necessary. He was absolutely certain that this was the right thing to do. For both himself and Miss Ellen. This would make her happy and more trusting of him, he was sure of it. He knew he had to make some grand gesture to win her over.

"Is that not something the woman arranges anyway?" Edward snapped. "I do not think it is something we should be discussing."

"The woman's *family*," Arthur reminded his father. "But her father has only just passed away. She is not going to be prepared to arrange a ball. It must be us, Father. Would it not be worse to let the occasion go by with no celebration at all? Will other people not find it very strange if we do not hold a celebration of the engagement?"

Arthur was not going to back down, and his father evidently saw it. It was almost a relief when he leaned back in his chair and gave a short, sharp nod. It wasn't exactly an enthusiastic agreement, but it seemed to Arthur that it was assent. The engagement ball was going ahead.

CHAPTER 13

HORSES WERE MUCH EASIER to deal with than people; Ellen had always thought so. Their needs were so simple, so easy to meet, there was never miscommunication or confusion. She did not need to worry about how she came across to horses.

That was why Ellen had spent all the time when she was not in her bedroom with the horses. It was a way for her to hide away from the expectations of her sisters as well. Gracelyn, most of all. But of course, Gracelyn was not the sort of person to be ignored for too long.

"Ellen!" she called across the field, anger dripping off her tongue as she moved with speed closer to her sister. Ellen knew she could not simply keep staring off into the distance, ignoring Gracelyn, for much longer. "Ellen, you have been hiding from me, when you know we must talk. You cannot avoid the inevitable. We cannot just pretend yesterday did not happen."

Ellen sighed to herself before she finally turned around and looked into her sister's eyes. She had been hoping to avoid the confrontation for as long as possible, but it seemed the time had come. She was going to have to address it one way or another, whatever she finally decided. Did she tell her sister her plan to feign madness and include her in it? That didn't seem the wisest thing to do. Alternatively, she might try to continue to manipulate her sister with the deceitful plan.

She did not like the latter idea, but it seemed the only thing she could do.

"I do not know what you are talking about," Ellen replied with a soft little smile as she continued to pet the horse. She tried to seem absent-minded, as if she really had no idea, but Gracelyn could see right through her.

"You do not know what I mean?" Gracelyn's face darkened. "You jest, Sister. I have never seen you act the way you did in front of the Maxwells earlier—in front of the marquess. It was absolutely humiliating. I did not know what to say. I am surprised the offer is still on the table at all after the way you behaved. It was very odd."

"I—" Ellen shrugged helplessly, not sure what she should say. Perhaps she should have planned her answer before starting the discussion, so she would not have found herself in such a tricky situation.

After all, there was no excuse for what she had done. Not one she could guarantee Gracelyn would believe at any rate. Her sister had always been far too clever.

Gracelyn groaned as if she was in true agony. "Oh no, please tell me you are not planning something. I cannot go through *that* experience again."

Panic coiled through Ellen—panic because her sharp-witted sister was already catching on to everything she was planning. She supposed she had not been very discrete with her behavior. Gracelyn must have been terribly confused about everything Ellen had said as she stood by the window, speaking nonsense about rabbits and rain drops. It was a miracle she had not challenged Ellen at the time.

"I do not think it matters," she said instead, attempting to change the subject, "because I have been thinking things through, and I still believe we can make things work without accepting the duke's offer."

Gracelyn huffed in dismay. "So, we are back to that? I thought you had realized this marriage is the only way out. I do not understand why you seem to have changed your mind all over again. We decided that because it affects us all, we must make some smart decisions, but now—" She threw her hands in the air in dismay. "Now I do not know what to say to you. I do not understand what you are thinking. Why can you not simply stick to our original decision and just get married?"

"But to the marquess?" Ellen screwed up her nose. "I do not like the duke; nor do I appreciate the pressure t he is putting on me to make the decision so quickly."

"He is doing that because he knows we will not get a better offer, Ellen. He knows that if we do not accept his, we will fall into destitution. He has a good understanding of the way that money rules the world, and he holds that over us. I know it means he will have the land, but that is all we have to offer. Although it's in a parlous state, and we would be lucky for anyone to buy it."

Much as Ellen wanted to snap at her sister not to be so melodramatic, she chose not to. She bit her tongue because this was not how she wanted her plan to go. The idea was not for her to fall out with her sister by going against her wishes, but to seem to be going along with them—until the marquess rejected her as a marriage prospect.

"I do understand what you are saying," Ellen finally replied. "And I do know there is a great deal resting on my decision. It is simply hard for me, that is all. Much as I do not wish to refuse this opportunity or jeopardize our futures, it is terrifying for me." Gracelyn did not seem to understand that at all. "I suppose it is because it has come so soon after Father's death. I am reeling from it. In truth, I have not been feeling like myself at all."

Gracelyn opened her mouth, as if she was about to argue further, but thankfully, whatever she had been about to say fell unspoken. Instead, her expression softened.

"Perhaps I have been a little harsh," Gracelyn admitted. "And I do understand how challenging this has all been for you. Losing Father, and then this . . . proposal; it is a lot. Joy has been telling me over and over that I have been selfish."

"I do not see it that way—" Ellen tried to interject, but she did not get far.

"I will try to behave more sensitively. Speak more rationally to you about things. I do not want my temper to drive a wedge between us," Gracelyn said.

Now it was Ellen's turn to soften a little. She fought with Gracelyn often, but they usually made up naturally, without talking much about it. She had never seen her sister express so many emotions all at once.

"Your temper will never drive a wedge between us," she insisted. "We are family. We will always have one another. You must not worry."

They shared a moment of understanding, an honesty they had not shared in a very long time. Ellen had built her internal walls up high, trying to protect her sister from knowing the truth about what she really thought and was planning to do. Gracelyn must not find out about Ellen's plan, for to do so might cause a family fallout that could never be mended.

Even if Gracelyn was a little suspicious, Ellen was sure she could talk her out of it.

"I am terribly sorry again for my misbehavior," Gracelyn said with a smile. "I shall go inside now and let Joy know she need not keep hiding—that things are fine between us."

Ellen and Gracelyn laughed together, happy in one another's company for the first time in what felt like forever. It transported Ellen back to a time where life had been so much simpler and their relationship not under such strain. Guilt flooded Ellen as she considered again the damage she might cause with her secret machinations.

She knew she was risking a lot with her plan, which really seemed quite silly when she thought about it. There was the potential to lose absolutely everything, but the worst thing would be her sisters' love. They would survive, somehow, without the duke's money, she was convinced of it. But without one another, they would not find life easy at all. They needed each other. They were the only family left to them. It was essential they stick together through anything life threw their way, including this.

Once Gracelyn was out of sight, Ellen breathed a little easier. It was suffocating being around someone she loved by had to lie to when she really did not want to. In fact, Ellen did not like lying to anyone. She'd even felt guilty putting on her little display of madness in front of the marquess. He did not seem to be the same terrible man as his father, but that did not change a thing. She'd had to behave as she had for both their benefit.

Arthur Maxwell did not really wish to marry her, she was sure of it. Just as much as she did not wish to marry him. She'd caught a glimpse of relief in his eyes the moment when she postponed the proposal for just a little while longer. That had seemed genuine, and therefore, was probably not due to her lack-witted pretenses.

"Oh, Father," Ellen whispered as she leant her head against the side of the horse. "I need to know I am doing the right thing. Again, I find myself doubting my actions. I keep thinking that this whole plan is madness. Madder even than I'm pretending to be. Oh, I do not know—"

She tried her hardest to blink back her tears, but Ellen could not contain them. A few cascaded down her cheeks, filling her with a deep sadness. Everything was a reminder of how alone she truly was.

CHAPTER 14

PLANNING A BALL WAS NOT EASY. Arthur had not thought it would be a completely straightforward exercise, but he was certainly not expecting to feel so overwhelmed as quickly as he did. The event had to be absolutely perfect, or his father would lose his mind.

The duke had made it very clear that he did not want to have anything to do with the engagement party because he did not trust Miss Ellen Greenfield. Nor was it even certain that his plan for the marriage was going ahead as he wished. But Arthur was determined. He was sure the ball was exactly what Miss Ellen needed to cement her agreement.

Luckily, his father had been spending a lot of time closeted in his bedchambers recently—probably to escape the planning stages for the event. *The thought of all that expenditure is probably making him ill,* Arthur mused.

"Oh, my goodness." Arthur tugged his fingers through his hair. "This is so hard."

"Is there anything I can do to help you?"

Arthur jumped. He had not realized he was not alone. He had been so caught up in his thoughts and worries, he had not heard his trusted friend, Rose, enter the room. She might be a servant, but Arthur enjoyed her company. She had always been there to offer him comfort through may difficult times, including the death of his mother. *Perhaps she might help me now too?*

"I am planning a ball to celebrate my engagement to Miss Ellen Green-field," he explained. Despite the strange way she had behaved on his recent visit, pride still surged through him when he thought about marrying the beautiful Greenfield sister. "She is still under a lot of strain and feeling very sad because her father only recently passed away."

"Oh, that is terribly sad," Rose agreed, "but how nice it is that you have decided to do something so lovely for her, my lord."

"I hope she agrees, Rose," Arthur replied, "But, in truth, I am struggling with the arrangements. This is not my area of expertise. I do not know what to do make the event memorable for her."

"I am surprised your father is not more involved in the plans." Arthur's expression darkened, likely showing Rose everything she needed to know. "Well, I have assisted with the planning of similar events many times I the past, so my services may be of use to you."

"You will help me?" Arthur gasped in joyful surprise. "Really, Rose?"

"Of course, my lord, if you would like me to." She smiled. "I know what the ladies like."

Now, that was exactly what Arthur needed. Someone who understood what made a great ball, someone with the understanding of how to make such an event unforgettable for the lady concerned. Arthur felt Rose herself likely harbored dreams of a making a good match and even holding a glorious engagement party to celebrate it. Arranging his engagement ball might be something she could throw herself into as if it were meant for herself. Yes, Rose was the perfect person to help him.

"What is this?" The duke's voice boomed through the room, immediately darkening the atmosphere. "Son, are you asking the servants to help you with this engagement party of yours? Do you think that is wise?"

Rose did what she always did in such situations. She curtsied and scurried from the room, escaping before she could get caught up in any trouble. Arthur wished he could do the same thing, but he had no choice but to wait it out.

"I do not see what the problem is, Father," Arthur replied coolly. "Surely, it matters not who assists me, as long as the ball comes off perfectly?"

His father made a disparaging noise. "It is supposed to be a magnificent event. You want to capture the attention of the *ton*, do you not?"

"And *that* will happen, you may be sure." Arthur was not backing down. He was not going to let his father squash him again, especially not when he was refusing to help plan the event.

"Do you not think the future bride should be involved?" The duke snapped. "Or is the reason why you have not asked Miss Ellen to plan the event with you because you are uncertain as to whether she even wishes to be your bride? Because, as I have already expressed to you, I do not wish to spend a lot of money on a waste of time. It will be humiliating for all of us."

Arthur swallowed back a thick ball of emotion that lodged in his throat, though he was confident that Miss Ellen would eventually agree to be his wife when she saw how much he cared about her and all that he would do for her.

"We shall not be humiliated, Father," he insisted as strongly as he could manage. "All will be well. You will be successful in your dealings with the King because of gaining the Greenfield land, and I will have my wife. You do not need to worry."

"Hmm, so I am supposed to put all my trust in you?" Arthur shifted uncomfortably under the scrutiny of his father's gaze. Distrust showed clearly on the old man's pale face. "I do not know if that is something I should do. You have not yet proven yourself worthy."

Arthur tutted and shook his head as he watched his father walk away from him, leaving him to stew. There was something about his father's speech which had struck him; Miss Ellen might wish to be involved in the planning of the ball. He realized he should at least ask her. He should visit her again and find out if she was agreeable to his plan to hold a ball and if there was anything specific she would like to feature at the event. Perhaps a certain theme, or a specific type of flower for the decorations, or some particular music that she liked? Whatever she wanted, Arthur pledged to himself to bring it about. The ball should be all about whatever made Miss Ellen happy.

He must call on her again, without his father, of course. Even if it got him into more trouble, he must go alone—because this was to be *their* engagement ball. The duke's participation—apart from paying the bills—was not required.

~

Arthur's heart sank as he laid eyes on the Greenfield estate once more. The more he looked at the desolate, unplanted fields, the more depressing it became. The unused potential of the land was truly striking. The beautiful pastures, the gorgeous architecture of the house, the lovely location

—why, the estate really could be made stunning once again, given a bit of money.

What a shame that money, or the lack of it, had such a malign influence on nature's rich potential. It was not right. It was something Arthur wished he could change.

It was with a heavy heart that he stepped out of the carriage and knocked on the door of the house. Guilt almost crushed him as he stood waiting for an answer. He did not feel like an angel coming to save the ladies. How could he, when he knew what his father's ultimate goal was? It was all about money in the end....

But his own motivations were pure. He hoped Miss Ellen would come to understand that.

It was Joy who opened the door. The youngest of the sisters seemed surprised to see him and cast about warily to see if the duke had come also. Seeing he had not, she looked relieved and smiled at Arthur. She immediately informed him that Miss Ellen was at the stables. He should go to find her there. Joy gestured to indicate he should go around to the back of the house to find the stables, apparently untroubled by the thought of he and his sister being unchaperoned.

But *it's probably for the best*, he thought, following the gravel drive around the house to the rear courtyard. *This way, they could talk in private. Maybe that had been part of the problem as well. All this was such a lot for anyone to deal with, and she was probably quite overwhelmed.*

But outside, away from the house, with nature surrounding them, at the stables among the horses, things might seem a lot less threatening.

As he walked, Arthur caught the sound of rushing water—a small stream bolstered by the recent rains surged through the grass, keeping it lush and green. The life-giving water seemed to promise a better future for the land.

Water was indestructible and resilient. Arthur liked that; he needed that reminder. He wanted to be as indestructible as the water, and as resilient too. He needed those qualities now more than ever, in the face of his father, while all of this was going on.

A voice floated on the wind, capturing his attention. He could not hear what was being said, but he recognized the voice all too well. It was Ellen, presumably talking with one of her sisters. His heart fell; what a shame.

So, it would not just be the two of them. Still, he mustn't be too upset about it.

It might be as well to have the opinions of all three sisters about the engagement ball. Indeed, Miss Ellen might feel more comfortable speaking about her wishes with them by her side.

"Father, I still do not know what to do—" he heard Miss Ellen whisper into the wind. "I wish this decision was easier to make—"

Oh! Arthur stopped in his tracks, peeping into the stables, where Miss Ellen stood by one of the stalls. *But Lady is not speaking with one of her sisters after all. She's actually talking to one of the horses, and she's calling it 'Father'. Hmm... ?*

"Miss Ellen," Arthur had to speak. He needed to find out what was going on, perhaps because the lady had behaved so strangely the last time they'd met.

"Oh, marquess! How wonderful it is to see you." If Miss Ellen was surprised to see him, she did not show it. "I am so grateful you are here."

"Likewise, my lady. May I ask what you are doing?" Somewhat taken aback and plunged into uncertainty once more, Arthur approached her and pointed towards the horse.

"Oh. Yes. Well, what I mean to say is that your visit is timely. Because you see, now you two can meet one another." Miss Ellen cocked her head to one side and smiled at him. It was a beautiful smile, no doubt about it, but it left him feeling confused and uneasy.

"I see. By 'you two', I assume you mean . . . me and . . . the horse?" he asked, almost laughing at how ridiculous he sounded. Of course, if this was her favorite horse and she wanted to introduce him to it, then that was perfectly fine. However, he had the strange sense there was something more to it than that.

"Of course." Ellen beamed. "I did not think this opportunity would come so soon—not after what happened with your father. But here you are, and things have worked out absolutely perfectly. I am so very excited!"

Arthur gulped nervously—and waited with bated breath for what the lady would say next.

CHAPTER 15

"FATHER, this is the Marquess of York, Arthur Maxwell."

Arthur could not believe his ears or his eyes. He blinked a few times, but the scene in front of him did not change. Miss Ellen really was introducing him to the horse as if it were her father, not simply her favorite steed. Oh, dear.

"I'm s-o—s-sorry," he stammered awkwardly, "would you please tell me the horse's name once more? I think I might have misheard you—"

"Of course," Miss Ellen replied with the utmost sincerity. "This is my father," she supplied, stoking the horse's nose, "and he is very excited to finally have the opportunity to meet you. He did not think that chance would ever arise, which is why this is so perfect."

Oh, dear indeed. That smile—it's so sweet, so innocent. Miss Ellen really does seem to believe every word she says.

Arthur parted his lips as if about to speak, then shut them again. There was so much he wanted to say, but he simply could not find any suitable words. What sort of response did she expect, he wondered? Would it be better for Miss Ellen if he simply went along with her—delusion? Or should he simply politely point out that this was a horse before them, not her father?

Everyone grieved differently; that much he was sure of, but this seemed to be on another level. This was an extreme reaction to loss by anyone's standards.

The horse neighed, breaking the awkward silence of the moment. Miss Ellen leaned in, positioning her ear close to the animal's mouth. Arthur sucked in a shaky breath, anxiety gripping him as he watched her nod understandingly, as if she comprehended the horse's meaning.

"Oh, my dear marquess, that is wonderful news." Miss Ellen pulled back and smiled at Arthur. "He believes you seem to be a fine young gentleman, and he would like to become better acquainted with you. Especially if you intend to marry his beloved daughter."

Arthur let out an anxious laugh. "How very amusing, Miss Ellen, to be sure." He hoped this was all a joke. "But you do not need to try and impress me with your sense of humor. I already admire you greatly."

Miss Ellen's face turned to stone. Her spine stiffened, and her eyes narrowed in his direction. If that was not bad enough, her lips twisted in to a thin, angry line. She might as well have had steam pouring out of her ears.

"I do not know what that is supposed to mean," she said icily, in a voice he had not ever heard from her before. Offense rolled off her tongue with every word. "It is a great honor to meet my father. And certainly, it is not a joke. I thought you would more respectful when meeting him for the first time. I am gravely disappointed, I must own."

"Oh, I apologize, my lady, er, Mr. Greenfield. I was under a—a misapprehension. I am, of course, delighted and honored to meet your father." Despite himself, Arthur found himself bowing to the horse. He simply wished to placate Miss Ellen, who was behaving even more oddly than the last time. Much as he wanted to be understanding of her apparently fragile state of mind, which was quite understandable in the circumstances, things were becoming increasingly challenging by the moment.

Miss Ellen nodded graciously, as if forgiving him for his *faux pas*. "Very well. So, I imagine you would like to have some time alone to discuss things with my father?" Miss Ellen cocked her head to one side curiously. "To discuss the possibility of our marriage. Is that not what usually occurs at this stage in the proceedings?"

Arthur nodded; he did not know what else to do. Of course, he did not wish to be left alone to discuss anything with the horse, but if he did not agree, he feared upsetting Miss Ellen again.

"I shall take a walk, then, to allow you both some privacy," Miss Ellen declared as she backed away from Arthur. "I will not be far away, so do call me when you have finished speaking." She turned and left the stables.

Arthur gulped. He was afraid that if he called her back, he might blurt out all the things he was trying his hardest not to say.

Once he thought Miss Ellen was out of earshot, Arthur turned back to the horse. He eyed it curiously, half-expecting it to speak and introduce itself as the Greenfield patriarch. Of course, it did not. The horse was not Miss Ellen's father. It was just a horse. The poor lady had chosen it as the repository of her temporary madness brought on by sorrow. She simply did not wish to accept that her father was no longer alive.

"I understand," he whispered to the horse. "Such a loss is hard to bear. I do not wish to be without my mother either. But such losses are something we all must learn to accept in this uncertain life."

But how best could he help Miss Ellen with her affliction? What could he do to make her feel better? And what if her—madness—persisted?

Arthur hated to admit that his father might be right about anything, but what if he correctly saw more than Arthur did in Miss Ellen's nature? There was a reason why his father did not trust the Greenfield sisters. Arthur had assumed it was because the old man was on edge about completing his plan to obtain their acres and pleasing His Majesty, but now... ?

Well, now he could not help but wonder if his father was not on to something.

"What shall I do?" He murmured to the horse, now extremely worried. Plus, to add to his concerns, from where he stood, he could see Miss Ellen dancing and skipping about the courtyard as if she was a six-year-old child rather than an adult woman planning her marriage.

He actually wished for one of Miss Ellen's sisters to appear, so that he could perhaps get some information from them about their sister's behavior.

One thing was certain, he was not going to be able to speak with Miss Ellen about the ball, as he had hoped to do. Now, he simply wished to leave. This meeting had only made him even more anxious than he had previously felt.

Perhaps this is altogether wrong, and I should not have come here at all? Perhaps I should pull out of the whole thing, to allow Miss Ellen time to get better?

He got no answers from the horse. Arthur stood in silence for a few moments, stroking its nose, wishing for a solution to come to him. But none did: He was simply more confused than ever.

"Have you finished your conversation with my father?" Miss Ellen suddenly reappeared next to him, making him jump. "How did it go?"

"Erm, it went well," Arthur improvised. "But unfortunately, I must take my leave. I only called in on my way to London—I have business to attend to there."

"Oh, you do?" Miss Ellen smiled, apparently not concerned by the prosect of him leaving. "Well, of course, I understand. You have business. I am simply grateful that you were able to meet my father today. He greatly appreciates meeting you and gives us his blessing, which is all one can ask. I hope you are looking forward to our wedding as much as I am."

So, there is going to be a wedding. She has decided. But Miss Ellen seems to go back and forth on the subject, first claiming to need time for us to get to know one another, then—this. It's all so very confusing!

But Arthur did not want to pursue his concerns just then. He simply wished to make his escape. However, he could not go right away because he could see in Miss Ellen's eyes that she wanted him to say farewell to her 'father'.

The horse.

And, since he had already gone so far along with the madness and wished not to upset the lady again, he did not feel he had any other choice but to fulfill her wish. Even if it made his heart sink. His conspiring with her delusion was likely not helping Miss Ellen, but, at this point, he felt it was not his place to judge or make any rash decisions.

He was going to take the easy road out, even if it felt utterly wrong.

"Well, thank you so much, Mr. Greenfield." Arthur bowed to the horse and patted him on the head. "I appreciate all your kind words. And thank you also for allowing me to court your daughter. I truly think she is a wonderful lady."

Miss Ellen smiled at him, clearly pleased, but Arthur felt truly dreadful. He hated feeling the need to escape from her when the sight of her tugged at his heart strings. But he truly did need to leave her because, while he was with her, she made his brain all foggy and confused.

"Good day, my lady," he said, bowing and turning away from her to walk quickly out of the stables, guilt flooding him with each parting step. Arthur honestly had no idea what he was going to do, what his next move should be. He was more confused than when he'd arrived—and he hated that fact.

CHAPTER 16

OH NO!

Ellen did not feel good at all as she watched the marquess walk hurriedly away from her. But wasn't this was what she was aiming for? The reason why she was putting on the whole charade? Yes, but she did not like it one bit. After all, none of this was his fault. He seemed to be trying his hardest with her, and he also seemed to be a very nice gentleman.

But now she had surely pushed him away. With her spur-of-the-moment decision to pretend the horse was her father, she had surely pushed him away once and for all.

But was that what she really wanted? Sometimes, it seemed as if she *needed* to push him away, and at other times, she yearned to have him close. It was all so very confusing, like a battle raging within her, and she did not know which side would win out.

Maybe I'm simply driving myself mad? Whatever the truth, her heart ached as she watched him leave. A big part of her wanted to stop him, to explain, to apologize to him. She wished she could explain everything, just to make him understand. Perhaps he would even smile that lovely smile of his and reassure her that he completely understood why she was doing whatever it was she was doing.

It had occurred to her that the marquess seemed to understand that his father was a terrible man. He did not seem to be anything like the clearly money-hungry duke. The confrontation between father and son in the parlor the other day had shown signs of the marquess being quite different to his father, and even somewhat frightened of him. Maybe if she gave him a chance, he would turn out to be kind and prove his worth as a husband. If she really gave him a chance and truly got to know him, as she had promised to do, then she might at last see the proof of his goodness.

But that was not something she would ever be able to find out. It was too late for that. The marquess was walking away, and quite possibly, he would never come back.

"That is what I wanted," she whispered, shrugging her shoulders as he vanished out of sight, her chest burning with pain now that he was gone.

This is what I have been trying to achieve all along. I cannot be upset about it now. I cannot change my mind.

But even as she continued to stroke her horse, the guilt crashed over her in endless waves. The feeling shook her to the core. She was not quite sure what her next move was going to be. She felt frozen to the spot, completely stuck.

Ellen did not like to deceive people; it was not in her nature. Whether it was people she hardly knew, such as the marquess, or people she truly loved and cared about, such as her sisters. She had gone back and forth on her decision to manifest insanity, and now she was struggling with the choices she had made.

But after that little show, it was likely far too late for her to step back. She could probably not return to trying to show the marquess her real personality. He had no idea who she was by now, and likely, he did not want to find out more. Why should he?

"No, I have started digging that hole now," she whispered as she leaned her head against the horse, who was blissfully unaware of his recent trans-formation into her father. "If I try to pull myself out of this hole, I might push my sisters further in to it. I might even lose them," she told him.

The hole was already very deep, and Ellen realized she could not see out of it anymore. The more she tried to think about it, the more she felt trapped in it, scraping at the walls with no chance of escape.

She sucked in several deep breaths, standing still, debating everything once more. She felt as if the world had descended onto her shoulders, sucking out every scrap of energy. Her plan might have seemed like a good idea in the middle of the night, when the light of the moon had shone so mysteriously upon her book shelf, but the reality of executing it was proving very different—and altogether quite unpleasant.

Eventually, she looked away from the horse and stepped out of the stable to scan the dying landscape surrounding her. The fields looked dead. The great trees no longer looked so grand, with their branches broken, their roots tangled and twisted. The sight broke her heart all over again. She wanted to save her father's land, to justify his years of hard work, to ensure his legacy lived on. *But what if I lose it all instead and just made things ten times worse?*

A strange sense of doom overcame her. In a sense, she supposed she almost resented the ruined estate, for the corner it had painted her into, for dying right in front of her eyes. The pastures where she had once gamboled with her sisters now seemed like a far-off image in a crystal ball. Nature, like her father, was passing away. It was utterly heart- wrenching to witness it, knowing there was nothing she could do about it.

"Why do I feel so compelled to keep on fighting?" she wondered aloud. "All I am doing is bringing hardship and worry to my family. Ever since Father passed away, it is tearing us apart. We are ruined. And it only gets worse every single day. I am starting to worry that we will never escape this horrible place we are in. I fear that nothing will ever be the same again."

She slumped to the ground, not worried about crumpling her dress. She did not care if it got muddy; she was too consumed by sadness to worry about it. *Pretending to be insane is really draining me!*

None of her books had warned her that her trickery would have such terrible effects. If they had, she might have changed her mind and done something else entirely.

"I do not have the energy for this fight anymore," she whispered. "I do not have the energy for anything anymore. I do not know if I can keep on going. I feel that I should give up and simply forget it all."

One day, she thought, I'm going to regret this moment. She would look back on this day and know she had made a grave mistake. That would be the moment when Gracelyn would chastise her and remind her that she had told her all along that they needed the marquess for their very survival. That the duke's cold-blooded offer was the only one she would ever have.

If she was still here in many years' time, still standing amid the estate's dying land, living in destitution, with absolutely no money to support them, then it would come home to her, she was sure, just what a terrible mistake she had made in driving the marquess away. Her sisters would likely be gone by then, that was, if they managed to find themselves husbands to look after them, if her supposed madness had not ruined their prospects and meant that no suitor wanted to go near the Greenfield family.

Ellen's green eyes began to tear up. But these were not the same tears she had been fighting off for days. They were more like the tears she had been unable to hold inside at her father's funeral. They came surging down her cheeks like a stream, which made her clutch at the dying earth, gasping for air. The crying fit was unbearable and completely unexpected. Crying this for her father was understandable, but weeping this way for the marquess, whom she did not even know, made no sense.

Deep down, Ellen knew she was crying because she was scared for herself and her sisters, that she was worried about making the wrong choice. But she was also sobbing because of the marquess. She hated hurting him and pushing him away. That pained look in his eyes as she'd forced him to speak to her 'horse-father' had been so intense. It had made her feel so terribly guilty. She hated being the one to inflict that sort of pain on him.

"What was I doing?" she sobbed, glad no one else could see or hear her. Thank goodness everyone had taken to leaving her alone. She could sob as much as she wanted. As if she could ever feel better for it, though.

Why did I ever start this lunacy? I truly must have lost my mind.

The house felt a million miles away. She could not even bring herself to rise to her feet, never mind walk back to the house. And what was the point of returning anyway? By putting her silly plan into action in secret, she was sure she'd pushed her sisters away as well. Gracelyn had been growing increasingly angry at her, and it was starting to get to the point where Joy could not look at her either. Ellen had noticed how her younger sister avoided her eyes whenever they were close, which was not like Joy at all. They had always been close; even when she'd fought with Gracelyn, she and Joy had always had a special connection.

Ellen broke into more tears. She leaned her head on the ground, probably muddying her hair as well, just to add to the mess that was her life, and she wept some more. At this point, she was not sure she was ever going to stop.

CHAPTER 17

SHE HAD no idea how long she had lain on the dead grass weeping, but it must have been a long time because her eyes were burning hot, probably extremely red, and her head was pounding with a headache. Still, Ellen did not want to move, but it was starting to feel like she must. After all, she could not remain where she was forever.

It took her far too long to get to her feet and much longer to start walking. It was probably for the best, really, because Ellen wanted the redness in her eyes to calm down before she got inside. She did not wish her sisters to see her in such a state; they would worry about her even more than they already were.

The one thing Ellen hated more than being dishonest was crying in front of the others, having to receive their sympathy. As the oldest sister, Ellen was supposed to be the one looking after everyone else. She could not stand the idea of the girls having to take care of her. That would certainly not make her father proud.

No, crying was supposed to be a private activity of self-reflection, not a cry for attention, to make Joy and Gracelyn start talking to her again. Ellen made sure to circle the house a few times before she headed inside. The more time spent calming down her skin and burning eyes, the better. She finally slipped in through the front door, thankful that no one was there to see her. Ellen could not hear a sound as she tiptoed through the hallways.

She checked each room as she walked past, just to try to see where the girls were, but she seemed to be alone. That was something she was used to by that point, since the home was much too big for the number of people living in it, but it felt strange, nevertheless. Ellen could not put her finger on it, but something felt odd, as if a strange, dark cloud floated through the house. . . .

It is just me, she tried to convince herself as she ascended the stairs. *I am the one with the problem. All the crying has made me very sensitive, that is all it is.*

Ellen headed towards her bedroom, her head down, with purpose in every step. She needed to check the state of her dress in the mirror, to see how muddy she had made it. Her hair and face as well. She was going to have to properly clean herself up.

But she did not quite make it all the way to her chambers. Whispered voices caught her attention, sounding strange in the odd silence shrouding the house. The sound caught Ellen's attention, and she could not stop herself from creeping closer to listen in to what was being said.

"Joy, you know this is something we must discuss," Gracelyn hissed coldly. "We cannot put it off any longer. Otherwise, we do not know what will happen."

Ellen's heart nearly stopped beating. Now she absolutely had to continue listening.

"I do not wish to discuss it with you, Gracelyn," Joy shot back. "Please."

"So, we are just going to allow Ellen to continue behaving as she has."

Ellen's blood ran ice cold. She did not like the bitterness in Gracelyn's voice. Of course, her sister had caught on to what she was doing, Ellen had tried to prepare herself for that, but now the moment had come, she felt distinctly umprepared.

"Our sister is under a lot of stress," Joy reminded Gracelyn. "You know she has not taken Father's death well. I think it is hurting her—"

"I do not agree," Gracelyn interjected. "In fact, I believe our sister is using her grief to manipulate the marquess and the duke, to prevent the wedding from ever happening."

Joy was silent for a moment before she responded. "How can you say such a thing, Gracelyn? That is terrible. Ellen would never do that. It might not be the love story she has always dreamed of, but she has agreed to marry the marquess, to ensure that we can be secure financially and have good lives. I even think she might like him. He does not seem like such a terrible gentleman as his father."

Ellen swallowed back the guilt, or at least she tried to, but it was impossible. It remained lodged in her throat, making it hard to breathe. If she was not careful, she would grow dizzy through lack of air.

"He might well be the nicest man on the planet, who is offering dear Ellen the most wonderful life style, but she is not going to take it," Gracelyn sneered. "Have you not noticed how she stays in her bedchamber all the time lately, no doubt trying to avoid us because she knows she is doing something wrong?"

Joy said nothing. Ellen could not blame her for that because Gracelyn had described exactly what she had been doing. "And then saying all kinds of mad things when the marquess is here? About the rain and the rabbits? About our father?"

"I do not think. . ." Joy attempted to say, but Gracelyn was not going to let her speak.

"Joy, you are being naive! Look at the way she scratched herself all the time the marquess and duke were her the last time, as if there were spiders biting her or something. I thunk she is trying to pretend she has a disease to push him away."

Ellen clapped her hand to her mouth to try to stop the gasp from exploding from her lips. Of course, Gracelyn had noticed every detail of what she had been doing! The sharpness of her sister's mind had always been going to be a problem. Ellen had not thought her plan through as much as she should have—just another regret to add to the ever-growing list.

"I believe it is the grief," Joy persisted, which was terribly sweet, Ellen thought. She had been worried she was pushing her youngest and closest sister away, but Joy was still on her side, no matter what. "I think we are not giving Ellen enough credit. She is upset, heartbroken. Plus, she is the eldest sister, responsible for the pair of us. And this so-called marriage proposal on top of everything else . . . I am not surprised if she's acting a little out of character. We should help her, not condemn her."

"Oh, Joy, you are so naive." Gracelyn tutted loudly. "Why I should have to explain this to you, I do not know, but you can be sure that Ellen does not need our help. She is not struggling. She knows exactly what she is doing, and if we do not do something about it, then our lives are going to be absolutely ruined because of her. Is that what you want?"

Guilt crushed Ellen. She wanted to run into the bedroom and apologize to her sisters for everything. She wanted to promise them both that she would be a million times better in future, doing whatever they wanted her to do to make it up to them. All she wanted was for them to be close once more because the terrible feeling of loneliness would eat her alive if she let it.

But there was something stopping her. Something that would not let her move: Ellen knew she was in too deep. Even if she tell her sisters all, Gracelyn would never forgive her. It was too late.

"So, if that is the case," Joy finally asked, "then what do you suggest we do about it?"

Ellen groaned internally. Gracelyn had twisted Joy's opinion around to see her side of things. Ellen had lost her, too. She had known she would eventually. There was no possibility of Joy resisting Gracelyn's argument forever.

"I have a plan." Gracelyn sounded pleased with herself as she loudly announced it, but then her voice sank low once more. Ellen had to really listen hard to hear what was being said. She was not sure if she was glad to have done so or not, as what she found out was horrible. "Because I do not trust Ellen to do what is right, I am going to marry the duke myself. That way, we will still be able to save ourselves financially."

The duke?

Ellen staggered backwards as the words took hold. She tried her hardest to understand their meaning, but they would not seem to sink in.

The ruthless duke could not marry Gracelyn. No. That was not at all what Ellen had intended when she embarked on her plan. This was not supposed to be the outcome. If Gracelyn managed it, then Ellen would never be able to forgive herself. She would know she had pushed her sister into danger, just to protect herself. Her father's land was not worth her younger sister's happiness.

What on earth was she going to do now?

CHAPTER 18

ARTHUR DID NOT KNOW what to make of the duke's mood or his slightly green complexion. His father seemed both pensive and strange, which made him feel anxious. He kept wanting to speak during their carriage ride to the Greenfield estate, but he was not quite sure what he should say. He didn't want to vex his father before they even arrived.

Perhaps he had gone too far, insisting on this engagement ball, but he was certain it was the right thing to do; he just knew it.

"I do not trust this family," Edward commented, almost under his breath but loud enough for his son to hear. "If it were not for the land, I would have nothing to do with them."

Arthur gritted his teeth, trying not to react to his father's baiting, but he simply could not stop himself. Something had to be said, no doubt about it.

"They have not given you any reason not to trust them."

The duke gave Arthur a chilling look. "What about the eldest girl's refusal to agree to the proposal immediately? And still she shillyshallies. What about the fact that you have shared secret meetings with them behind my back? It is very strange."

"They do not have their father around to depend on, Father," Arthur tried his hardest to be reasonable, but of course, it was a pointless action because the duke simply did not want to hear it. "It is probably not the time to expect normal behavior."

"Humph," the duke shot back dismissively, as if Arthur was far too young to understand the ways of the world. At that moment, though,

Arthur was sure he understood some things far better than his father did. He certainly felt as if he could see things more clearly than the old man.

He could only hope now that his father was not outright rude to the Greenfield girls. They had been through enough; they did not need that again as well.

Upon arriving at the house, Arthur quickly noticed that Miss Gracelyn was already standing by the open front door, a friendly smile upon her face. Arthur was a little unnerved by that, but he could not think why. There was absolutely no reason for him to be distrusting at all. Miss Gracelyn had not done anything to make him feel that way, yet he could not seem to stop himself.

"How wonderful it is to see you again, Your Grace, Marquess," Miss Gracelyn greeted them, curtseying politely. "Thank you so much for coming to see us again. Please, come inside. Tea is all ready for us in the parlor."

If the duke found the change in Miss Gracelyn strange, he did not show it. He seemed happy to follow the young lady to the parlor, where young Miss Joy greeted them. Miss Ellen, Arthur noticed as he and his father sat down, was nowhere to be seen.

"Miss Ellen will be joining us shortly," Miss Gracelyn informed them. "She has been riding. She has been spending a lot of time with the horses recently. I believe they help soothe her grief somewhat."

Arthur wondered if he should mention that Miss Ellen was possibly spending a little too much time with the horses. One specific horse, in fact. But he decided against it. It would do no good for the duke to find out that his son's future bride thought her own deceased father was a horse.

The duke was unpleasant enough as it was, and Arthur did not want to do anything to make things any worse than they already were.

Joy brought in the tea and cakes, handing around teacups and plates of sweet delicacies to the company. They made stiff small talk to pass the time, and Arthur noticed Miss Gracelyn was talking an awful lot with a forced sort of cheerfulness. And most of it was being directed at his father.

Clearly, the lady was very keen for the matter of the proposed match to progress. To Arthur, it seemed plain that she understood the situation as perfectly as the duke. She knew, as her elder sister seemed not to, that this was the best chance the sisters were going to get.

But Arthur did not wish for his marriage to be thought of as merely a business arrangement contracted over a few acres of land. He wanted things to be much more romantic for himself and Miss Ellen, because he was sure that would be the best possible start to their future together.

"Your Grace, I insist that you try one of my father's cigars," Miss Gracelyn was telling the duke. "They have such a wonderful aroma, you know, admired by many."

Before the duke could reply, she had risen to her feet and went to bring over to him the box of fancy-looking cigars. Arthur had never been interested in smoking himself, so it did not impress him at all, but the duke's eyes lit up.

Any sign of his underlying irritation suddenly dissipated.

"Well, it really does look as if your father had excellent taste in cigars."

"Please, take one," Miss Gracelyn insisted. "I am sure he would be happy to know you are enjoying one of them."

Miss Joy looked down at the floor. Arthur could not be certain, but it seemed to him that she was not as keen on the idea of the duke smoking her father's cigars as her sister was. Since she clearly felt she was in no position to object, Arthur stepped in on her behalf.

"Father, perhaps it is not a good idea for you to smoke a cigar just now." The duke glared at Arthur, vanity clearly clouding his judgement. "I am only thinking of your health. Cigars are not good for you, now that you are getting on in years."

"Thank you for your concern, son, which is completely unnecessary. I think I can decide when I may smoke a cigar without your help," Edward snapped back, while Miss Gracelyn cut the cigar for him and went to fetch a light. "Perhaps you would do better to recall your purpose for being here instead."

Arthur almost argued, but before he could do so, Miss Ellen finally made an appearance. Her ethereal beauty shone out from the doorway, causing Arthur's pulse to begin pounding with happiness. She was absolutely beautiful, so flawless and lovely. Arthur thought that he could look at her all day long. . . .

At least, that was how he felt until she parted her lips and let out the most ear-piercing scream he had ever heard in his life. In his shock, he even covered his ears with his hands to attempt to protect his eardrums.

Miss Gracelyn and Miss Joy both jumped up to help their sister as she nearly fell to her knees. Whatever was troubling her mind was clearly consuming her all too quickly.

"He is not Father," she wailed, so loudly that Arthur could hear her despite his attempts to block her voice out. "He should not have the cigars. Father will see."

As Arthur lowered his hands, a suspicion suddenly overcame him. Why should Miss Gracelyn give the duke a cigar if she thought Miss Ellen might react so violently against it? Surely, she had seen glimpses of her sister's encroaching madness before? She must know how her older sister was struggling.

So why the cigar?

It did not make any sense!

Unless. . .

Arthur could hardly breathe as an outrageous notion filled his mind unbidden. Was it possible that Miss Ellen was hiding something from him and his father? That there was a lot more to the situation than met the eye?

Arthur wanted to move closer to Miss Ellen, as her sisters had done. To hold on to her shoulders and stare deeply into her emerald-green eyes. He wanted to ask her to be open and honest with him, to tell him what was really going on. He felt that would be the key to getting the truth from her.

But, of course, that was not something he could do while they were surrounded by everyone else. Her sisters would not like it, and his father would certainly have a lot to say about it.

So, he had to sit exactly where he was and wait until her sisters managed to calm the afflicted lady down. However, he knew he must get Miss Ellen alone soon, to ensure the opportunity of them having an honest conversation. He had a feeling that he would learn a lot from it.

"I am truly sorry," Miss Ellen finally gasped as she eventually took her seat. "I should not have had that outburst. It is simply—strange to see another man smoking one of my dear Papa's cigars."

That was the duke's cue to stub the cigar out, but he ignored it. Instead, he simply blew out a haze of smoke, nodded his head in evident satisfaction, and pointed the cigar at Arthur.

"My son has an announcement to make," he declared coldly. "I think it might be best if he made it now."

The girls all turned to stare at Arthur expectantly. He was struck by the pain in Miss Ellen's eyes. It did not feel at all like the right time for his announcement. In fact, he thought, they should postpone the whole idea, but it was too late now. His father had put him on the spot.

"I have been arranging a celebration," Arthur announced in a slightly trembling voice, looking at Miss Ellen. "To celebrate our engagement." Miss Ellen's eyes flew wide with surprise, but Arthur knew he had to continue. "It is a ball, which I think will be a wonderful way for us to impart the good news as well as a very enjoyable event for us. I actually have invitations with me, if you would like to look at them."

"Oh, my goodness," Miss Gracelyn said, sounding pleased. "How thoughtful of you, marquess. That is, indeed, wonderful news. I'm sure we should love to see the invitations."

Miss Joy could not keep the smile off her face either. Arthur could almost see her imagination running wild as she considered dancing at what was probably one of her very first balls.

Miss Ellen remained impassive, and it was impossible to fathom what she was thinking. But that did not trouble Arthur too much. It did not matter to him that she might feel uncertain just then because he was going to do everything in his power to ensure that she had a wonderful time at their party.

And if he could use it as an opportunity to get her alone, to attempt to find out the truth about her, then that would be even better.

CHAPTER 19

ELLEN PLANNED on causing a scene from the very first moment she'd learned that the duke and marquess had arrived. She had done a good job so far of sowing the seeds of doubt about her sanity in the mind of the marquess. Now, she simply wished to drive that point home.

However, the sight of the duke smoking one of her father's cigars had truly affected her in a way she could not control. The last time she had seen anyone with a cigar, it was her father, when they'd shared that conversation about his health.

Of course, it could not have been that one last cigar which had pushed him over the edge. There was nothing anyone could have done about the heart attack, but she was always going to feel the guilt. She would always wonder if she could have done more to save him.

What if she could have saved him somehow? Then, she would not be in this mess at all. He would still be here, and everything would be perfect. She would not have the weight of the world pressing down on her shoulders.

Ellen was not sure she would ever be able to forgive her sister for offering up their father's cigars to the duke. It felt like a step too far in their already fractured relationship. Ellen did not wish to lose her sister forever, but she was starting to wonder if it was inevitable.

A light tapping on Ellen's bedroom door alerted her to her youngest sister's presence. Joy's was a face she did not mind seeing just then.

"Ellen, may I talk with you sincerely?" Joy asked as she stepped inside.

"I suppose so," Ellen agreed. "But I cannot talk for too long. My headache is terrible. I feel like there is someone screaming going in my head."

It was much harder for her to keep up her little acts of insanity in front of her sisters, especially Joy, but she could not only perform in front of the duke and marquess; that would seem far too suspicious.

"Screaming?" Joy's lips turned down into a frown. "I see. That is troubling."

Ellen's blood ran icy cold. "Whatever do you mean?"

"I feel you are not being honest with me, Sister, and it hurts me very much."

Guilt flooded Ellen once more. It was almost overwhelming. She fell backwards onto her bed, staring at Joy with fear in her heart. Her youngest sister's questioning eyes pierced through Ellen and made her melt.

How on earth was she supposed to keep this up when, as the oldest, she was supposed to be the protector? Especially since their father had passed away. But that was not what she was doing, was it? She was actively hurting her sister with her acting. It was not right. Ellen did not know what she was supposed to do.

"Please," Joy begged. "Just be honest with me. That is all I am after."

Ellen leaned forwards, getting closer to her sister. "Can you keep a secret?"

Joy rolled her eyes. "Of course, I can. What do you think? I simply wish to know what is happening with you and how worried I should be about you. I am tired of being seen as the youngest, the naive sister, who must always have her feelings protected."

"I do not—" Ellen started, but Joy held up her hands to silence her.

"You do that all the time. Both you and Gracelyn. But I am a grown woman, and I can handle anything as well as you both can." She sniffled a little, a sudden sadness seeming to come upon her. "After all, I have been living with the knowledge that Mother's death was my fault for my entire life. I am sure nothing can be as bad as living with that."

Ellen was so stunned she did not know what to say. "What are you talking about, Joy? Mother's death had absolutely nothing to do with you—"

"She died giving birth to me. Of course, it was my fault."

Ellen gasped and clapped her hand to her mouth. She could not believe her little sister, the one with the sunny disposition, was secretly holding so much pain inside. The realization overwhelming for Ellen.

"Joy, you cannot blame yourself for being born. That is not something anyone asks for. It was not your fault."

"But I know that you and Gracelyn must blame me. You must."

While Ellen could not outrightly speak for her sister, she decided she must in that moment because Joy did not need ambiguity in this case. She needed to hear something absolute to make her feel better.

"Joy, Mother was a very kind woman," Ellen told her sincerely, "with a very big heart. But she was weak and sickly. She could not manage the birth, yes, but that is not your fault, and I do not wish you to hold onto this blame any longer. Gracelyn and I have certainly never felt that way about you. We love you, and we would not change a thing."

Ellen rose and enveloped her sister in a hug. Joy almost collapsed into her arms and clung to her sister as if she was the only thing keeping her upright. How painful it was to Ellen to discover that Joy had been hurting for such a long time. She knew she must do better for Joy in future. She absolutely must.

"I am so sorry that you have been so burdened," she told Joy, intensely moved. "I will try my very best to do something to make you feel better."

"There is something you can do," Joy's eyes narrowed. "You can tell me what is going on. I know the subject has changed, but my curiosity remains. I would like to know what you are up to, even if it must remain a secret."

"I do wish I could tell you," Ellen admitted. "But I am worried about burdening you further. If I tell you, then you will have to carry it with you too."

Joy rolled her eyes once more. "I know what you are trying to do. You will not 'burden me' because of what I can see it with my own eyes—you do not wish to marry the marquess. Your odd behavior is a sham. You are using it to try to push the marquess. I can only assume that, for some reason, you think it will be better if he rejects you rather than the other way around."

"I—" Ellen could not deny it. Perhaps Joy was just as sharp as Gracelyn, but she simply had not noticed up until then.

"But I do not think that is going to happen," Joy continued, not giving Ellen a moment to make an excuse. "Because while you have been trying to put him off, he has been planning an engagement ball for you. It seems to me that he likes you and wishes to marry you despite your little act."

Ellen's chest grew tight. Joy was right. The news of her own engagement ball had come as a huge shock to her. She was not even sure what to think of it. She had been gracious as she took the invitations from the marquess to inspect them, and she hoped she had managed to seem excited about the ball. But truth be told, she'd been in a spin thr whole time.

"I believe he only wishes to marry me for the land," Ellen said, once more hoping to get Joy on her side. "I do not think it has anything to do with me."

Joy reached out and held Ellen's hand reassuringly. "I am not sure about that, Sister. I know this might not be the fairy tale romance you have always dreamed of, but that does not mean it cannot become that. I have a feeling that the marquess might be just the right man for you. He seems caring and kind. He could treat you very well."

Ellen wanted to disregard that, but Joy was only voicing the thoughts she herself had already had. Arthur really did seem kind, even if his father was the opposite. She truly did feel their union could turn out to be something wonderful—but there was always the chance she was quite wrong about that, and her life would be utterly miserable with him.

"I am afraid," she whispered to Joy. "I am worried about changing my life so drastically. I am scared that I will end up losing the only family I have ever known."

Joy nodded understandingly. "I know. I would be afraid if I were in your position as well. But this is a change that we will all have to make at some point in our lives. Even if Father was still alive, you would have gotten married one day."

Ellen's eyes welled up. It was hard for her to accept that. "When did you become so wise?" she laughed with Joy. "You do surprise me."

"I told you, I am a grown woman," Joy reminded her. "I am capable of much more than you give me credit for. I hope you can see that now."

"Oh, I absolutely can see that, you do not have to worry."

Underestimating her younger sister was not a mistake Ellen would make again in a hurry. Joy had changed her mind completely. Just as she was about to tell her as much, Ellen's bedroom door swung open, and Gracelyn came storming inside.

"What is going on?" Gracelyn demanded. "I thought we were a family.

What is this secret meeting between you two? What are you hiding from me?"

Ellen could have argued that Gracelyn had instigated meetings with Joy without her, to talk about the wedding, but she kept her lips clamped shut. Gracelyn was clearly looking for a fight; that much was obvious by the flames dancing in her eyes. But Ellen did not want to give it to her.

"So come, fill me in." Gracelyn flung herself onto Ellen's bed. "I want to know exactly what you have been talking about. It seems very important, with all this whispering going on. . ."

Ellen and Joy shared a look. Something was happening, something unpleasant was in the air. It was almost as if a bomb was about to explode, leaving destruction in its wake.

CHAPTER 20

"So, you are not going to tell me?" Gracelyn snapped, bitterness lacing her tone. "Well, that is fine. I do not need to know what you are talking about because I am sure it is very boring. Compared to *my* news, anyway."

Gracelyn stared at her sisters expectantly, but neither Ellen nor Joy answered her. Ellen was not sure she wanted to know what her sister had to say anyway. It was surely going to be hurtful, otherwise she would not be so thrilled.

Why must her sister take such delight in being so cruel?

"I am sure you are both terribly interested," Gracelyn continued, not at all bothered by the awkward silence filling the room, "and you certainly will be when I tell you what is happening." She giggled and announced, "I am getting married."

"Married!?" Ellen could not hold herself back. Of course, she'd already overheard Gracelyn's ludicrous whispered proposal, but if Gracelyn was now saying she was to be married, then it could be more than just a pipe dream. "What do you mean, you are getting married?"

"To the duke, of course." Gracelyn's eyes shone with delight. She was enjoying herself. "So, whatever it is that you are up to, you might as well give it up. It does not matter. The plan is going ahead. The duke will receive the estate as my dowry, and I shall become his duchess and live in luxury for the rest of my life."

Ellen was utterly bewildered. She could not believe what she was hearing. Gracelyn was talking about it as though it was the best thing that could ever happen to her.

Joy was not so silent, though. "The duke has agreed to marry you?"

"We have had a lovely conversation," Gracelyn answered. "He is quite taken with me, apparently." She flipped her hair over her shoulder. "He thinks that I am truly beautiful. His wife passed away many years ago, so he has been longing for a new duchess to grace his arm. I fit that mold exactly, do you not think?"

Ellen and Joy continued to say nothing, until Gracelyn became visibly enraged at their silence.

"The marquess commented on my looks as well," she continued spitefully, "he said that I am the most beautiful Greenfield sister. I am quite sure he would rather marry me now, anyway, after the way Ellen has been behaving. Perhaps I shall make him *my husband* instead."

Ellen knew that Gracelyn was trying desperately to provoke her, and she did not want to give in to it, but she was no longer in control of herself. She felt an unexpected pang of jealousy kick at her. It was not at all a nice feeling.

Gracelyn noticed Ellen's pain and jumped on it immediately. "So, I shall be a Maxwell soon, whichever one I decide to marry. Whether it is the duke or marquess. Life is going to change for me."

"Is that really what you want?" Ellen folded her arms across her chest in defiance. "For your life to change? Are you so miserable with the way things are?"

"Do you think I should be happy here? In a miserable home, on land that is dying all around us. I do not wish to remain here for the rest of my days. I want to live."

This broke Ellen's heart in two. Their father might have been used to the girls fighting because their personalities were so different, but Ellen was sure this would be too much even for him if he were still here.

"So, you are saying that the life Father created for us here is not good enough?"

Gracelyn rolled her eyes. "Father is not here any longer. He would not want to leave us here, either. He would want us to be happy. You should know that, since you have been talking to him all this time."

Ellen froze. Gracelyn knew more than she had realized. Perhaps she truly had been engaged in a private conversation with the marquess, in which he had told her about the incident with the horse. If that was the case, then he probably had expressed his desire to marry Gracelyn rather than herself.

She did not like it; it made her stomach sink, although she was not quite sure why.

It must be Gracelyn. Ellen was upset because of their complicated relationship, nothing more. It could not be linked to the marquess; he was simply collateral damage, caught in the middle of the sisters' conflict.

If he married Gracelyn, then he would always look at Ellen like the poor, mad spinster sister. The same would occur if Gracelyn married the duke. Ellen was going to have to do everything she could to make sure no weddings took place.

"Nothing to say, Ellen?" Gracelyn taunted her sister. "I do not understand. There is no screaming, no talking to yourself, no signs of madness at all. . . ."

"Why are you being like this?" Ellen demanded. "Why do you have to be so cruel, Gracelyn? You make it so difficult for us to get on, and I am really not sure why. I do not understand why you must always argue with me."

Gracelyn shrugged and smirked. "Maybe that is for you to decide, not me."

"No, I do not think that is the case." The more Ellen talked, the more excited she became. "Because it is not just me who suffers from your sharp tongue. I do not ever see you with friends, even at social events."

"That is because I do not like the snobbish girls who attend those events, as you well know, Ellen."

"Is it?" Ellen moved closer to Gracelyn, seeing red. "Or is it because you cannot seem to get along with anyone? And now you are talking about marrying a much older man, purely for his money title? No one will like that."

"You think I will trouble myself about the whispers of others?" Gracelyn snapped. "I shall be the one married to a wealthy duke. It will not matter what anyone else thinks. I shall not worry about any of them."

Actually Ellen knew that was probably correct. Gracelyn had likely gotten used to the idea of being friendless In fact, it might turn out to be a life where she thrived.

"It would not be right." Even Ellen knew it sounded weak as she said it.

Gracelyn tossed her head back and cackled. "The duke thinks I am beautiful. If he should want to marry me and make me a rich duchess, then how does that affect you? I am doing what is right for me. I do not know why I am even telling you this. It is not as if your opinion means a thing."

Ellen glanced over to Joy, who was now sitting in the corner, all color drained from her cheeks. She had lost the ability to stand up for herself, so Ellen was going to assume the responsibility on her behalf.

"You think this will not affect me and Joy?" she snapped at Gracelyn. "What about losing the land our father worked so hard to keep for us?"

"Again! Must we keep repeating the same argument? The land is *dead*." Gracelyn snorted. "Better for the duke to have it and put some money in to it rather than us merely continue to watch it die. You are so selfish, Ellen. How can you not see that? Joy, please tell Ellen."

Joy said nothing. She sank further in on herself, panic in her eyes. Neither sister was going to reach Joy now. Not that either of them should have been trying to pull her one way or another. It was not fair for her to be caught in the middle of their arguments.

Unfortunately, Ellen was the only one who seemed to understand that.

"Joy, will you say something?" Gracelyn yelled. "Ellen is going to kill us just so she can hang on to the land that our father allowed to die. It is going to ruin our lives, and she selfishly refuses to admit the truth. Please, explain it to her."

"She does not want to!" Ellen exploded, throwing her hands in the air in frustration. "Because she does not agree with you. Stop trying to put words in Joy's mouth. I cannot believe your actions, Gracelyn. You have always been very difficult and unpleasant, but this is the hardest conversation I have ever had to have with you."

"You are being unpleasant also!" Gracelyn was not going to back down. This fight was clearly what she had been angling for, and now she had gotten it. It was a fight that had been brewing between the sisters ever since the duke and marquess had entered their lives, but Ellen still did not wish to fight. All this only left her more upset than before.

"You are being stubborn, Ellen. You are making things impossible for Joy, and for me. All we want is to have some financial security—and you are ruining the chance for us."

Ellen shook her head, trying her utmost not to let the tears come spilling out. The last thing she wanted to do was show weakness while Gracelyn was like this.

"You are a traitor, Gracelyn," she snarled instead, storming from the room; she simply could not stand to be in the same room as Gracelyn any longer. "You are a traitor who does not care about our father at all. I cannot stand you."

As Ellen stormed out, she could hear her sister yelling behind her, but she did not let her words sink in; she was too busy letting her tears fall once more. At this rate, Ellen thought she would dry up completely and have nothing left inside.

Surely, life was not supposed to be this hard, this painful. Ellen was certain she was not supposed to feel so lonely all the time. She was not sure how to fix things, or if she even could.

CHAPTER 21

ARTHUR FELT he was bubbling inside, literally stewing in his anger. Never had he felt so much rage in his life. He was red hot and did not know what to do with any of the feelings overwhelming him. It was all too much. He felt he could erupt at any moment, like a volcano. It was almost impossible for him to contain himself.

This visit to the Greenfield estate was supposed to have been a pleasant one. He had thought the announcement of the engagement ball would make Miss Ellen happy and bring her closer to him. Instead, he now felt as if he knew her less than ever.

Who was that woman? What was she hiding from him? He so desperately wanted to know what was going on. But now, his father's behavior was making him even more unsure of what was going to happen next.

"Ah, I am so grateful to get acquainted with Miss Gracelyn," the duke sighed, completely oblivious to the mood in the carriage. "Now, she is a wonderful woman. I am sure her father must have been very proud of her."

"What about Miss Ellen and Miss Joy?" Arthur shot back, refusing to allow them to be overlooked. "Do you not think their father would be proud of them as well? They are lovely young ladies."

"Pft," Edward scoffed. "I find them both too quiet, and the eldest daughter is very strange. That behavior about the cigar was abhorrent."

"She was upset. Those were her father's cigars."

"And her father is not around to smoke them anymore," the duke pointed out, as if speaking to a child. "I do not see what the matter was; I was a guest in her home, an honored guest. I am the Duke of York. I was offered the cigar. I should not have to witness that dreadful display. What a scene. That is not the way a lady should behave in front of anyone. What is wrong with her?"

"She is grieving."

"You cannot use that as an excuse for everything. Nor can she," his father insisted. "There are times when you are expected to behave in a certain way, and when you have guests in your home, that is one of those times. She was ill-mannered today, just like the youngest sister. Now, Miss Gracelyn; she is the shining star in that family."

Arthur screwed up his nose in disgust. It had not escaped his notice that Miss Gracelyn had been flattering his father, nor that the duke liked it. As if his life was not complicated enough, now he was going to have to consider the possibility that his father might actually take someone like Miss Gracelyn as a bride.

But that could not happen if he was already wed to Miss Ellen, could it?

Although the way things were going, he was not sure that marriage to Miss Ellen was going to be a smooth ride. It all depended on what she was hiding from him. If it was all manipulation, then he would not like it and might even have to walk away. But if it truly was due to her sorrow at losing her father, then he would work with that.

That was what he would discover at the ball. One way or another.

"You are acting as if you are thinking of marrying her, Father," he commented cautiously. "Please tell me that is not the case."

Edward bristled. "Why should I not consider marrying Miss Gracelyn?"

His heart sank. His father really did look as if he thought it a good plan. Arthur knew his father had been growing impatient with Miss Ellen dragging her feet over the decision whether to marry him or not, as well as her strange behavior, but he did not need to take such a drastic step as to marry her sister to obtain th estate!

"In fact, it is a good idea to consider making Miss Gracelyn my wife," the duke continued, rolling over any of Arthur's objections before he could even think about expressing them aloud. "Since it is all too obvious we cannot trust Miss Ellen. I am not even sure that young lady wants anything to do with you."

The statement was like a dagger in Arthur's heart. He feared the same thing. He was starting to see that Miss Ellen was doing everything she could to push him away. He simply had not wanted to admit it to himself. However, his father had forced him to do so with his terribly cruel words.

"Miss Gracelyn is far too young for you," Arthur insisted instead. "Everyone will gossip about your very young wife. And anyway, you have never made a good husband, have you? Only a good businessman."

His father grinned from ear to ear, choosing to take it as a compliment. "Yes, now that is very true. But remember, Son, this is *about* business. It has nothing to do with marriage in a romantic way. After all, I must get my hands on the Greenfield lands somehow. I cannot fail. It is one of those chances that comes around only once in a lifetime. Once the King sees I have succeeded, there will be no more worries."

No more worries. Now, that was a concept Arthur could not even begin to imagine. He had always suffered from worry, and he assumed he always would. His father winning the King's approval was going to change that.

Once Miss Ellen truly accepted him, he would have a wife to try and keep happy, and if it turned out that she disliked him, then that was going to be truly problematic. That did not even consider his fresh concern that his father might marry Miss Gracelyn. Now, that was a match made in hell.

The duke might be impressed with Miss Gracelyn, but Arthur supposed it was probably because he saw a lot of himself within her. Arthur did not enjoy her company very much for that very reason. She had the same ruthless, uncaring attitude as his father did.

Those two being married would not be good for anyone, least of all him.

~

The moonlight bathed Arthur's bedchamber, which perhaps should have brought him some peace, but unfortunately, tonight was different. Arthur had no idea how late it was, but sleep was not coming for him.

Instead, he found himself tortured by worries about Miss Ellen. Truly, he could not work her out. She had seemed happy at the idea of a ball, and she certainly had not complained that he was pressurizing her, even if that was how it seemed. He was sure she would love what he had planned; with the romance of the beautiful music surrounding and the dancing, it would be perfect, he was sure.

But he remained a little troubled.

Arthur gave up trying to sleep and paced around his room instead, his thoughts speeding through his brain. It was all well and good telling himself that he could wait until the night of the ball to try and speak to Miss Ellen alone, but now, alone in the middle of the night, he was not so sure.

He was starting to think that, perhaps, it would be best for him to find out her true feelings beforehand, so the ball was not ruined by worries and doubts. If it was supposed to be the night when they celebrated their engagement, then finding out the true state of affairs sooner rather than later would be best.

Or perhaps that was merely his impatience speaking. Either way, he was convinced that by morning, he would be setting off on yet another trip to the Greenfield estate—without his father. No matter that the duke would disapprove.

Was Miss Ellen a master manipulator? Or was she losing her mind purely from grief? Right now, she was an enigma, a mystery, one which Arthur truly wanted to unravel to discover the truth inside.

Miss Gracelyn seemed rather sly, and Arthur was she had an unpleasant side, while Miss Joy seemed like a sweet ray of sunshine. It was only Miss Ellen whom he could not read. It did not help that his heart was clouding his judgement— because she was just so beautiful.

Yes, Arthur was sure he could not wait around any longer. He needed to know Miss Ellen was about, and he was going to have to go first thing in the morning, or he would never be able to sleep again. He was confused enough without adding exhaustion to his list of problems.

CHAPTER 22

ARTHUR'S HEART was racing as he traveled across the Greenfield estate to the stables to see if Miss Ellen was there. He found her inside alone, and he didn't think for one second about the rules of propriety.

He had slept a little but not enough. That was why he had not hesitated to call at the estate. He could not spend another night like that. He needed his rest so he could have a clear head, and this was the only way he could ensure that.

Arthur paused as soon as he spotted Miss Ellen in standing in the stable doorway. He waited for a moment so he could examine her from afar without her spying him. He wasn't sure exactly what he was seeking, but he wanted to see her behavior when she was not with other people, just in case it proved different.

Well, she certainly did not seem to be talking to the horse, as she had in front of him. She was ignoring her 'father' for the moment. But then, Miss Ellen was organizing the tack, so he could not really be sure. She appeared to be lost in the task at hand.

Arthur was struck by the sight of her as he watched her move gracefully about, despite the difficulty of the work she was undertaking. He felt the same sensation as when he had first met her: He couldn't keep his pulse calm in the face of her beauty. Never had he been so struck by anyone as by her.

What a shame that things had become so complicated.

Arthur allowed his imagination to wander a little as he watched Miss Ellen work. He lost himself in the fantasy he had created for himself when he very first laid eyes on her. He thought then that she would make a lovely wife and that they could be very happy together. He'd even thought at the time that she might like him too. There had been a look in her eyes back then that had struck him hard. He was sure he had not imagined it.

But her behavior had changed so much since that day, and it was impossible to figure out why. Remembering why he had come was about the only thing that got his legs moving, that got him walking towards her at long last.

Arthur was not sure if it was a good that Miss Ellen did not seem to sense him as he walked towards her. He almost wished that she would, so he did not have to announce himself. But that did not happen. Miss Ellen was far too engrossed in her work.

He had to clear his throat twice once he was in hearing distance to try and capture her attention. Since Arthur was not sure about her state of mind, he did not wish to do anything to frighten her.

"Oh, Arthur." Her eyes widened the moment she spotted him. "I did not expect you. This is truly a nice surprise."

She smiled, seeming to accept his presence with good grace, which was a huge relief. He did not wish to trouble her, but he needed crucial information.

"I hope you do not mind my calling unannounced," he said, just to check.

"Oh, yes, I am looking forward to talking about our engagement ball with you. I have been thinking about what to wear. Because, of course, we will all want to look our best."

Oh, that was a nice easy subject. One Arthur was sure all couples discussed before such a celebration. A smile spread across his face as he started to think there might not be a recurrence of the usual madness today.

"Have you anything in mind? In style, I mean. Of course, I am sure you have many beautiful gowns—"

His words trailed off as he suddenly realized that money, or lack thereof, might be an issue for the ladies. Clearly, the Greenfield ladies had been struggling to make ends meet for some time. They might not have dresses suitable for a grand engagement ball. Should he offer to take her shopping?

"No, silly," Miss Ellen giggled girlishly, her cheeks shining a pretty shade of pink. "I was not worrying about myself. I am thinking about my father."

Uh oh. Arthur deflated. This was not a normal conversation after all. His lips turned down into a frown as he watched Miss Ellen turn back to stroke the horse.

"Do you think he would look better in brown or navy blue? Father has been having a difficult time deciding for himself, and I simply do not know enough about male clothing."

Arthur found himself at a loss. Did he allow this to continue to placate Ellen? Or must he finally do what he had come here to do, however uncomfortable it made him feel?

Yes, he had no choice in the matter, did he? He had to.

"Miss Ellen, I must ask you about your intentions," he finally said aloud. "I do not wish to question you in this manner, but I am at the end of my tether. At this point, there is nothing more I feel I can do. I must ask you." She continued to stare at him blankly, as though she did not understand him. "Are you putting on an act? Behaving like someone who is mad to escape marrying me? If so, I would much prefer that you to tell me so outright."

Miss Ellen's gorgeous emerald eyes grew large and vacant. Regret coursed through Arthur's veins. He wished he had not said anything. But perhaps it was already far too late to take his words back. The damage had been done.

"I am terribly sorry for my forwardness," he continued, in a poor attempt to assuage at least a little of the pain he imagined he had caused. "I do not wish to upset you. I am simply attempting to discern the truth of the situation, which has become extremely painful to me."

Miss Ellen backed away from him. Suddenly, she darted out of the stables and raced out of sight, leaving Arthur alone. He did not think it was a good idea to follow Miss Ellen, in case he was playing into her hands further. Or pushing her away. But he had come for answers, and he could not leave without them. He was still uncertain about important matters, and he intended to resolve that uncertainty. Even if it caused more devastation.

With a deep, regretful sigh, Arthur jogged after Miss Ellen, and he found her not far away, sitting on the grass and picking idly at it. Eventually, Arthur knelt beside her and tried to catch her eye.

"What is the matter, Miss Ellen? I wish you would talk to me."

Miss Ellen remained silent for a few moments, head bowed. Then, she shocked Arthur by breaking down into tears that rocked her entire body. Much as Arthur felt it was a breakthrough, he still felt bad for her.

"I am terribly sorry. I did not mean this to happen. I simply wish to know your feelings so that I can understand my own."

"Everything is dying," Miss Ellen wailed, clutching at the dead stalks of grass with her fingers. "And there is nothing I can do about it."

The devastation in her voice struck Arthur hard. There was so much pain radiating from her, he could not stop his heart from dropping to his stomach. All he wanted to do was help Miss Ellen heal the terrible pain within her. He would do anything to help her, whatever it took. Before this, she had been so guarded, so cold with him. This was the first time he felt he had seen the real her.

And the real her was utterly beautiful. She was like an angel. It was hard for Arthur not to become overwhelmed by her loveliness, despite the tears and sobbing. He melted, instantly knowing he would do absolutely anything for her.

He knew a little bit about grief, surely enough to support her, to be a shoulder for her to cry on if that was what she needed.

"Miss Ellen, I understand," he whispered to her. "It is terrible. Everything you have been through is utterly dreadful. No wonder you are struggling. There is no right way to deal with grief, but one can sometimes rely on the people around us, those who truly care about, for support at such times. I would like to be one of the people whom you feel you can rely on, if you will let me."

As their eyes locked, the rest of the world simply melted away into nothingness. He knew this was probably not the right way to behave, but it didn't seem to matter just then. The way his heart was pounding, and the way his breath caught in his throat was intoxicating, an addictive feeling that he could not get enough of.

Finally, he thought he saw in Miss Ellen's eyes the connection he craved. Before he could stop himself, he reached to cup her soft, pale cheek in his hand. She did not move, and excitement fizzled through his entire body as he touched her soft skin. The connection that had been building between them overwhelmed him physically as well as emotionally.

Arthur did not even think about his actions, much less the consequences. He leaned his head in towards Miss Ellen's, happiness exploding in the pit of his stomach as she tilted her head up towards him. It felt like the most natural thing in the world to crush his lips to hers and claim her with a kiss.

The kiss was incredible, much nicer than he'd ever imagined a kiss could be. It only proved to Arthur what he already suspected; that despite all the strangeness surrounding them and the odd way they had been brought together, there was something special between them.

A real feeling, one that was wonderful—one definitely worth fighting for.

CHAPTER 23

THERE WERE FAR TOO many things to worry about for Ellen to even consider sleeping. She might have been lying in bed, resting, as the night sky took over, but there was no possibility of shutting off her thoughts completely.

How could there be when she was plagued by thoughts of what had happened in the pasture today? The kiss. The kiss that had turned her world upsidedown and sent chills down her spine at the same time. The kiss that she could not stop thinking of, however hard she tried.

Things could not have gone less to plan. Ellen was supposed to be pushing the marquess away. She'd wanted him to walk away from her so she would not have to do the deed herself. Today was supposed to have set the seal on her plans.

Calling the horse her father once more and talking about what he might wear to the engagement ball was supposed to make the marquess run a mile. She'd assumed that, just like the duke, his appearance came first, and he would shy away from associating with this mad woman in public.

She needed him to think that more than ever now, to prevent Gracelyn from putting forth her plan to try and create a connection between herself and the duke—or the marquess—whoever fell for her scheme first.

But it had all gone wrong. Instead of believing her story that she was mad, the marquess had called her out on her behavior. He had confronted her about her actions, letting her know he saw right through them. And then he had been far too kind to her as she broke down.

The walls she had so desperately tried to keep around her heart to protect herself from the kind marquess had come crashing down the moment when he touched her cheek. There was something so lovely about being held like that, being touched by someone who truly did seem to care about her. It made her melt, her heart flutter, made her breath stick in her throat—all in the best way possible.

And then, he had kissed her. Ellen's entire life had flipped on its head as soon as it happened. The foundation of her existence was whipped away from beneath her, leaving her spiraling into an abyss of—pure happiness. After her father had passed away, she could not have guessed it was possible to feel so much joy again.

It was a beautiful kiss, even better than the sort she'd only read about in books. If Ellen was waiting to be swept off her feet by a knight in shining armor, then, somehow, she had managed to find him. The situation bringing them together might be financially motivated, but she had never felt such a sense of genuine romance before in her life.

He had been kind to her afterwards as well. He did nothing to embarrass her or make her feel she had acted improperly. Arthur Maxwell, Marquess of York had been the perfect gentleman. If anything, it made her feel even closer to him than before.

But because she had been manipulating Arthur, it was hard for her to know if she could trust him. What if he was also manipulating her? Throwing in a kiss to convince her of his false regard? He knew she was inexperienced and that she would be taken by surprise. He must understand how it would affect her and that she would not be able to stop thinking about it.

Surely, he could not do all of that to her—and it was all a lie.

Much as it did not seem likely, since the feelings they'd shared had felt so genuine at the time, she could not be certain. That was what troubled her now. She was naive and inexperienced. What if he was using that to his advantage?

Since she had been lying to him, she did not have the right to be as annoyed with him as she would like to be. How could she even blame him? It was utterly torturous. If Ellen kept this up, she would never sleep again.

She needed another kiss. Only that would help her determine whether or not he'd meant it. She had been shocked by the first one. She had not known it was coming her way, so surprise had stunned her. But if she planned when the second one would occur, then she could take her time deciding if the kiss meant as much to him as it did to her.

The next time she was likely to see him would be at the engagement ball. Could she steal a kiss with him then? She was going to have to, in case Gracelyn took the opportunity to make her advances on whichever man she deemed appropriate at the time. The ruthless manner of her sister's behavior made Ellen feel very unsure. The duke might have the title now, but picking Arthur as her target would cause the most damage. It would all depend on Gracelyn's mood and what she wanted to achieve.

Ellen could not recall the last time she had known what was going through her sister's mind. It felt like a lifetime ago. Currently, all Gracelyn seemed to want to do was lash out and cause lots of pain. The closer she brought Ellen to tears, the happier she seemed to be, which was truly terrible. Ellen did not like it one bit.

If only they were closer. Then Gracelyn could have perhaps helped her through this challenging time. But it was far too late for that to happen now. This chasm would likely always remain between them. It was truly tragic. Ellen was at a loss at what she could do to make things right with Gracelyn. It did not seem like her middle sister wanted peace between them.

Ellen had already confided somewhat in Joy, but it had troubled her youngest sister far too much. She did not wish to trouble her further, to cause her youngest sister sadness when she was supposed to be her protector. Especially since today had made her even more ashamed of her decision to pretend to be mad.

It was a wild idea in the first place. She never should have done it at all. If only she had the ability to go back in time to change everything. Then again, what else could she have done? She was still stuck in a terrible position; a choice between her father's land and financial stability. That was never going to be easy. Ellen did not know what she should have done differently.

"What is going to happen at the ball?" she wondered aloud. "How am I going to cope when I do not know what is going to happen?"

There was another potential disaster she aso had to think about, and it was yet another problem with no easy solution. The Greenfield girls had not been invited to a ball in a very long time, and they certainly did not have the right sort of attire for such a grand occasion.

This would be the perfect time for the girls to go out shopping, to one of the lovely dressmakers on Bond Street, where ladies were dressed in the finest, most fashionable outfits in the country. The ball would be filled with the cream of Society, while the Greenfield girls would be in their old dresses, looking foolish.

Her hand clapped to her forehead, and she held it there for a while as all the thoughts threatened to consume her. The more she tried to escape the situation, the deeper she seemed to sink into it. It was as if she were stuck in quicksand, and the more she moved, the more stuck she became.

If she was not careful, she was going to drown in it. She would never be able to pull herself out, and she would lose complete control of her life. Then, how would she help her sisters? How could she ensure their lives were not ruined?

Even with Gracelyn behaving as she was, Ellen wanted her to be safe. She was simply afraid she did not have the power to make that happen. She was not good enough. Her father had died assuming Ellen would step up and do what was right. Had he been wrong?

CHAPTER 24

ARTHUR CLASPED his hands together in excitement as he glanced around the hall to see how well his ball had turned out. He had a lot to thank Rosie for. Thank goodness for her wonderful insights, especially since his father had not been helpful at all. Although he was not showing that now. The duke was well and truly playing the role of a gentleman who controlled of everything. He liked to act that way, and usually, Arthur could ignore it, but tonight he had to admit it was getting on his nerves. His father had not even wanted to host the ball, and now he was pretending he had arranged it all. When the Greenfield sisters finally arrived, Arthur hoped would feel a little better.

He would then have Miss Ellen to talk to, which was all he really wanted. Ever since that beautifully passionate kiss they'd shared in her pasture, he had not been able to get Miss Ellen off his mind. He had thought of her a lot ever since he first met her, but that had now intensified. However cold she tried to seem when she was around him, however much she tried to push him away with her "madness", there had been passion in that kiss. Real feeling. He just knew it. He could feel it. There was no pretending with her lips.

That kiss was perfect, absolutely beautiful, and it only proved to Arthur what he already knew. That there were some real feelings between them. He had never felt that way in his twenty-five years of life. That had to mean something. Now, he could not wait to see her again tonight, to see what her demeanor would be. Would she be quiet? Mad again? Or would she acknowledge that there was something between them, which was what he wanted?

"Well, good evening, Marquess," Lady Elizabeth Turner declared as she curtsied in front of him. "What a wonderful ball this is. You have done a wonderful job of organizing eerything."

"Oh, well, thank you." Arthur smiled and bowed. "Thank you very much. It is very good to see you, Lady Turner. And your dress is quite fabulous."

Everyone had come looking their best tonight. The beautiful colors and different fabrics swishing around the ballroom were eye-catching. It was lovely to know that all these people had made such an effort to come to his engagement ball, the ball that Arthur had, almost, organized all by himself. It made Arthur a very happy man.

Lady Elizabeth Turner was a staple in London Society. If she was not present at an event, then it was considered by many not worth attending. She knew it, as well. It was a miracle really that she had not yet been snatched up for marriage. Although, if the rumors were to be believed, she was incredibly choosy and had not yet settled on the man she wanted. Although, with Arthur, she had always shown a lovely temperament. Arthur suddenly shook his head as he realized where his brain was going. He was not actually considering Lady Elizabeth Turner, was he?

He had never pursued her before, nor had he ever wanted to. As beautiful and kind as she seemed, he had not thought of her as someone he might marry, but now, with her standing right in front of him, smiling as if he was the only man in the room, he was not sure if he had not been a little too hasty in overlooking her.

Perhaps the reason Lady Turner had not wished to marry someone else was because she was interested in him. Now, that would really be something. . . . But again, he had not been interested in Lady Elizabeth Turner, or any of the other ladies who had ever shown him attention.

They hadn't attracted him, not in the way he had been immediately inspired by the unusual Miss Ellen. He had rapidly grown very quickly attached to her in a way that had nothing whatsoever to do with his father's business intentions. In fact, Arthur realized, it would be better for him if he did want to court someone like Lady Turner because at least then he would not have to bear the guilt he was experiencing at having to go along with his father's devious plan to obtain the Greenfield's acres, however unwilling he was to do so.

"Are you taken for all the dances tonight, my lord?" Lady Elizabeth asked him with a twinkle in her eyes. "If not, might you find a space for me?" Guilt flooded through Arthur as he wrote his name on her dance card. As the host of the ball, he was expected to dance once with all the single ladies present; he was highly eligible after all, but he could not stop himself from feeling badly about it.

Truth be told, there was only one lady he wanted to have his arms around. Her newly revealed passionate side had gripped Arthur, and he did not know what to do with himself. He let out a little sigh, thinking about her, as always. If only things were simple between them, then Miss Ellen would be the perfect lady for him. It was a terrible shame that the circumstances surrounding them caused her so much difficulty in opening up to him.

Arthur had seen the intelligent, insightful side of her, which was magnified by her intense beauty, but that was hard to keep in mind when she was making him talk to her 'horse-father'. But she had all but confessed to him that it was all confusion, grief, and fear. A fear he hoped had been finally pushed aside when they shared that wonderful kiss. Self doubt plagued Arthur. He moved away from the ladies rapidly, to try and get his thoughts in order. He was so been looking forward to spending the evening with Miss Ellen and getting to know her better. He did not wish their night to be ruined because he had returned to questioning every-thing. Yes, things were more than a little confusing, but that was no reason to get all worked up. He snapped from his mental downward spiral just as it was about to claim him, as he overheard whispers from the guests. Nasty whispers about someone not being dressed in the same sort of finery as everyone else.

Arthur's heart immediately sank. He did not even need to glance up to understand who was being spoken about. There was only one family who did not have the sort of money to match up to everyone else, and without their father around to help them out, it had to be the Greenfield girls. It was relieving and upsetting all at once. Miss Ellen deserved to have all eyes in the room upon her, but not for such reasons. It angered Arthur to think of the London *ton* as being so shallow, but, of course, he already knew that about them. Just like his father, they prioritized money over everything else. He could not help but think the entire world would be a better place if that were not the case. Why could others not focus on the beautiful emerald-green of Miss Ellen's eyes, or the stunning softness that crossed her face when she smiled?

By the time Arthur finally managed to look up, he was incensed, his nerves on edge. Perhaps because as much as he would like to consider himself as being so much better than everyone else in the room, he was not. After all, had he not been talking to Lady Elizabeth Turner? Enjoying her pleasant company and even considering how easy things would be if he simply chose to be with her instead?

What a terrible a person he was deep down, especially as this was his engagement party to Miss Ellen. This was the night when he was supposed to be celebrating his union with her. He had a lot of making up to do. His father greeted the Greenfield ladies first, as if they were all very close. As if he had not been treating them as lesser citizens all this while, whom he was using merely to obtain their land. But the duke was not only thinking about winning the favor of the King just now. He was also very much considering his public appearance. He wanted to appear to be the perfect host for the night.

The Greenfield ladies all curtsied and greeted the duke cheerfully, but they did not have a choice in the matter. It was of utmost importance that they treated the duke as special. Everyone else had done the same also, whether they cared for him or not.

Arthur stood back and watched for a couple of moments, intrigued by the scene unfolding in front of him. He could not help but notice that Miss Gracelyn seemed especially pleased to receive a kiss on the hand from his father, a sight which truly disgusted Arthur. The Greenfield girls were already being talked about enough without adding *that* into the mix of gossip. Arthur knew he must reach the girls quickly, to ensure his presence was known. He wished to reassure Miss Ellen that he would not abandon her at any point. But as Arthur moved through the throngs of people, all doing their best not to make it obvious that they were staring at the scene unfolding in front of them, Arthur realized his heart was pounding and his nerves were getting the better of him.

The moment he stood in front of Ellen, it was almost as if his legs had turned to jelly. He did not even notice what she was wearing. How could he be worried about such a silly thing when he was staring into her lovely, inquisitive eyes?

"Good evening, Miss Ellen," he said, with a sweeping bow but an undeniable tremor in his voice. Arthur hoped his father did not notice it.

"May I say, you look utterly ravishing tonight?" he added, admiring her.

A blush crept up her body to brighten her cheeks at the compliment. There was no denying it, she had softened to him a little.

"How lovely it is to see you, too, my lord," she replied shyly.

Arthur reached out and took her hand in his. With his gaze fixed upon her, he pursed his lips and pressed them to the silky soft skin of the back of her hand. There was a promise surging between them, he could feel it. A promise that tonight would be monumental for them both.

CHAPTER 25

ELLEN COULD NOT CONTAIN the shiver trailing down her spine as the marquess's lips grazed the top of her hand. She had been missing his strong lips and the scent she associated only with him; tobacco, with a hint of peppermint. It was a unique smell that Ellen would only ever associate with the marquess, a scent she enjoyed all too much. She had even been dreaming about it. And now, he was here, right in front of her, making her pulse pound with delight.

That was why Ellen had come to the engagement ball tonight. As apprehensive as she had been to attend a social event where she knew she would not fit in at all, wearing a dress she knew would be regarded as dowdy compared to the other ladies gowns, she knew it would be lovely to see the marquess once more.

"You must join me for a dance," the marquess said, offering Ellen his arm. "I have been very much looking forward to your arrival."

"Oh. Of course." Ellen's eyebrows rose. She was not expecting to be swept on to the dance floor so quickly. She thought she might be given a moment to adjust to the grand surroundings, but it was perhaps for the best. If she was given too long, she might talk herself into a place of self-doubt.

"Yes, let us dance." Ellen had been taught how to dance at a ball like this; every well-brought-up girl was, but this was the first time she felt as if she had to put her knowledge into practice. Her heart was thundering in her chest, she was so nervous, and it was almost impossible to breathe.

But at least, she thought, with the marquess holding on to her arm so firmly, she could not fall down.

Thank goodness she had his strength to lean on. Once in the middle of the dance floor, the marquess rested his hands on her hips, immediately intensifying Ellen's nerves. She felt she could not get enough of this glorious, intoxicating feeling!

Unfortunately, as she rested her hand on his arm, something caught her attention. Oh no! It was Gracelyn. Of course, it was Gracelyn. Ellen had been worried about how her middle sister was going behave at the ball. She had been in strange mood all day long, making comments about the duke. The duke with whom she was now giggling, while coyly twiddling her hair around her finger, her eyes locked on his the entire time. The problem was, he was staring back at her as if she was the only woman in the room.

To them, it was as if no one else existed. The duke looked enthralled by Gracelyn as well, which did not make Ellen feel any better. It left a painful lump lodged in her throat. Nerves, anxiety, and anger as well, swept over her. Why must Gracelyn insist on behaving in this manner when she knew it upset Ellen so much? She could not have genuine feelings for the deeply unpleasant duke, could she? She did not know him well enough, and he had not shown any kindness to their family at all. Even if Gracelyn was as ruthlessly ambitious as the duke himself, it all felt like far too much to bear. "Are you quite all right, Miss Ellen?" the marquess asked her, bringing her attention back to him for a moment. "You missed a few of steps there—"

"Oh, I did?"

Humiliation consumed her. She was supposed to be on her best behavior to make up for her dowdy dress. But it seemed she could not even manage to get that right. "I am terribly sorry, my lord. This is all a little—"

"Is it too much?" There was a new tightness to the marquess's voice. "I do apologize. I thought you would like it. It was only ever my intention to please you."

Ellen tripped up once more. "I'm sorry! It is not that, my lord. I am simply a little overwhelmed, that is all." She focused hard on her steps, not wanting to make any more mistakes. "This is all very beautiful, Marquess. You must have worked very hard to organize it all."

"I did it for you," he said gallantly. "I want you to be happy. I wanted to celebrate our engagement because it is very exciting."

His words trailed off. Ellen could only blame herself for it. He must have sensed her hesitation. Ellen had never felt so confused; she no longer knew what she wanted. Or how she should behave around the marquess—

"Oh, my goodness." The words came spilling out of her mouth before she could stop herself.

Heat burned in Ellen's cheeks as rage swallowed her up. "What on earth is my sister doing? She is behaving terribly. I wish she would stop it."

"What is she doing?" Without missing a beat, the marquess kept on dancing, but he looked keenly in the direction where Ellen's eyes were fixed.

"It is . . . Gracelyn." Ellen did not like admitting that to the marquess, but she had simply reacted spontaneously. "She is with your father. Have you seen them together his evening? They seem awfully close."

Ellen did not know how the marquess felt about the duke and Gracelyn, but she assume it would not be favorable. Surely, if he wished to be engaged to her, he would not want his father involved with Gracelyn? But she knew her sister would do whatever she wanted. She was a determined individual who would not be stopped.

"Oh no." The marquess rolled his eyes. It was not the reaction Ellen was expecting. "My father is behaving terribly today. He is expecting the King to arrive soon, which, of course, will boost his reputation and sense of self-importance. It will be even better for him to have a young girl fawning over him. I imagine that is what my father is thinking about at this moment."

"Th-the King?" Ellen stammered. "The King is coming?" She glanced down at her dress, now hating it even more. The King must not see her dressed this way! No wonder everyone else looked their finest! Ellen was not at all ready for the occasion.

"Yes, the King has suggested he might attend." Ellen could not imagine anything more terrifying than looking the King in the eye. But she tried her hardest to keep smiling. She did not want the marquess to know how much she was trembling inside.

"But that does not help you, does it?" the marquess continued. "With your concern about your sister, I mean. Is she still talking to my father?"

Ellen nodded, her lips tightening. Not only was she angry at her sister for flirting with the duke but also for leaving poor Joy abandoned at the side of the dance floor. She stood there all alone, looking worried. Ellen decided she would go and stand with Joy as soon as the dance was over. She did not wish to dance with any other men, at any rate. She had only come to see the marquess.

"Yes," Ellen bit out. "She is ambitious. She will not rest until she gets what she wants. I do not like the way things are going at all."

"Well, my father is the same way," the marquess said. "He is very good at convincing women that he feels one way, but in reality, he always has an ulterior motive."

That caused Ellen's blood to run icy cold. What could the ulterior motive be? She supposed it was because the duke so desperately wanted the Greenfield land, and Gracelyn was the best route to getting it if Ellen did not follow through with the marriage to his son.

"I see," she muttered, almost to herself. The rest of the dance went on in silence because Ellen's head was spinning. She did not know what to think. After what the marquis had said, she felt a little less angry with Gracelyn and rather more worried about her. Did her sister know what she was getting herself in to? Was she aware she was being tricked by the duke?

The dance came to an end, causing Ellen to pull away from the marquess. Perhaps they would dance again that evening—the ball was to celebrate their engagement, and dancing together more than once would signal their union to the company—but was that something she wanted to do? Besides, she wanted to check on Joy, although she could not see her youngest sister anymore. Perhaps she had found someone to talk to.

"Do you mind—" the marquess took Ellen's hand, and she looked at him again. "—if we speak in private for a moment? Maybe outside?"

"Oh!" Ellen was far too curious, far too intrigued to ignore his request. Since Joy had gone missing, she was not immediately needed. "Yes, my lord, of course."

"I think we should go outside. You can see the gardens."

The gardens . . . just the thought of them made Ellen recall the last time she'd been outside and alone with the marquess, and the kiss she so desperately wanted to reenact. Was that about to happen? Was she about to experience Arthur's lips all over again?

The dizziness of expectation was all-encompassing. She nodded in excitement because, of course, she wanted to see the gardens. In fact, she would much prefer that to the stuffy ballroom. The ball was lovely, and the marquess had obviously worked hard on it, but she would always prefer to be on her own with him. She felt much more comfortable that way.

Ellen followed the marquess through the crowds of people, unable to meet anyone's eyes as she walked. She was sure all eyes were upon them. At least, all eyes save those not staring at Gracelyn and the duke. But Ellen was not going to worry about any of that just then: She might be about to feel the sort of passion she had only felt once in her life again.

CHAPTER 26

THE COLD OF the night whipped around Ellen, making her shudder. She wrapped her arms around herself and stepped out into the lush green gardens of the Maxwell house that the marquess had offered to show her. They did not disappoint. Stepping out onto the thick green grass, seeing the lovely flowers in the moonlight was magical. Yet the sight made Ellen feel a little sad.

The gardens here were a stark contrast to the land surrounding her home, the land Ellen felt so connected to because it was the only link to her father she had left.

She let out a little sigh, causing the marquess to turn to her. He looked concerned. "Is everything quite all right, Miss Ellen? You seem—a little distracted."

She did not wish to talk about her father tonight. Especially not since the "horse-father" incidents were still so fresh in her mind. It did not feel right to do so now, here at the ball which the marquess had thrown to honor their engagement.

"I was just thinking about the moon," she improvised instead. "The sun symbolizes familiarity, while the moon is a constant player in unfamiliar emotions."

She was not entirely sure what she was talking about, but it had felt right to say it. This time, Ellen was not purposely pretending to seem mad, although, she imagined that was how the Marquess would take it. That was not really what she wanted the evening to be about, not when the marquess was looking so devilishly handsome under the moonlight. His skin shone, his eyes sparkled, Ellen could not stop her eyes from drifting down to his lips. All she really wanted was to be in his arms, to feel his warmth against her body. But, of course, she could not. It was not proper.

Then again, she had not behaved as she should have up until now. She probably should not have kissed the marquess at all! And especially not as she was so confused. Was she simply trying to force feelings of affection for the man simply to ensure an easier life for herself and her sisters? Or was she really getting romantically swept away, so that attempting to continue to distance herself from the marquess made no sense at all?

Her father had agreed she should only marry for love. He adored her ideology. But what could she do if she did not know which way to turn? What if she was not sure? Was this was love— or convenience?

"We must talk," the marquess said, ignoring Ellen's comments about the moon and the sun. "Would you like to walk or sit? There is a perfectly lovely bench over there among the flowers." She would have loved to sit on the bench to talk, but Ellen did not think she would be able to sit still for even a moment. "Let us walk and talk."

That would be best, she thought. She did not wish for anyone to come outside and find them alone. They would have to get married then. She knew she would feel more comfortable if it was just the pair of them.

"It is such a wonderful night," the marquess said, taking her arm and starting to walk. They did not say anything for a little while, they simply walked and enjoyed the moonlight. Ellen knew she had been brought outside for something, and she assumed he would get to it soon enough. She did not want to push the marquess until he was ready to talk, being a little nervous about where the conversation might go.

"Miss Ellen, I would like to know something for certain," he finally said. "About your mental state. I know we discussed it somewhat before-hand, but I would like to be sure. Have you been lying about it?"

Ellen swallowed hard, trying her best to rid her throat of the lump that formed there. This was it, the moment she must finally be honest. She could not keep pretending any longer, not now the marquess had found her out.

"I have not exactly lied," she said slowly, the words heavy on her tongue. "But I have been struggling a lot, as I am sure you can imagine. Obviously, my grief played into it because I was missing my father. But it was also because I did not wish to be pushed into marriage. Well, forgive me for saying so, but not with someone like yourself, to be sure. Because .. . my first impression of you was not a good one."

"What was your first impression?" the marquess asked, clearly somewhat offended. Ellen was not sure she should tell him. Still . . . she had come this far. There was no point in holding back now. "I thought you were spoiled, entitled, and greedy. But perhaps I got that impression because of your title and your family—and your father."

Of course, it was because of his father. Yet Ellen worried she had been too honest—she did not wish to offend the marquess more than was necessary. He did not say a thing, but she could almost feel the intense thoughts darting through his brain. The marquess certainly did not look happy, that much was obvious to her. Perhaps she should not have been quite so truthful! Was this a good time to assume her role of madwoman? To pass her behavior off as insanity?

"I am not anything like my father," he finally said. "I am very upset that you would assume so. I have never been anything like him. I do not approve of his behavior either. I see him, I understand what he is like, and I do not like it."

Guilt rushed over Ellen once again. She had mis-stepped once more. She feared she was drawing dangerously close to a situation where, no matter what she said next, the marquess was going to walk away from her in utter disgust. And she would probably deserve it.

"I am so very sorry," Ellen gushed. "I now understand the mistake I made. I was too quick to judge, to think you are the same as your father."

"You would not wish me to place judgement upon you based on your sister's behavior, would you? When she is so ruthless."

Ellen gasped, a little shocked. Of course, that was not something she would like at all, yet it felt a little cruel coming from him so bluntly. But then, perhaps she had come across as just as cruel as well, when she'd said the same about his father?

"I understand what you are saying," Ellen replied, trying to keep her voice steady. "I see now that I was wrong. I would not wish you to feel bad because of my hasty judgement. I see now that you are very different." The marquess looked down at her expectantly, waiting for her to continue.

Ellen understood that she owed him the truth of her feelings at the very least. "You are sweet and caring, open and honest. You do not have the same priorities as your father."

Arthur nodded slowly, seemingly accepting that. "I am so glad you can see it. . . ."

He did not say any more, but simply continued their walk around the gardens. She was nervous, terrified, but something else was happening as well: Her heart was opening up, opening up like a flower to this man in a way she had not expected to happen. She was letting him in in a way she never thought she ever would.

"I have something else I wish to talk to you about," the marquess suddenly announced. "I have not just brought you out here to talk to you about the things that have been going on with me and you. I also want to let you know a little more about me and my life. Perhaps that will help you to see me a little more clearly. That is what I hope, at least."

There were so many things Ellen wanted to say in response to that, but she could not bring herself to say a word. Instead, she simply nodded, encouraging the marquess to continue. Her mouth had gone surprisingly dry.

"There is something that I do not share easily or with many people. In fact, I do not remember ever discussing it properly with anyone at all. But I would like to share it with you."

Ellen's anxiety shot up, wondering what the topic might be. Yet at the same time, her heart was flooded with a grateful warmth for his trust in her. She drew closer to him, leaning against him and holding his arm more tightly. He patted her hand.

"I hope you feel you can share anything with me. That is what I hope for. . . ." Ellen found herself saying. She had not been honest with him so far, but that was all going to change from now on. If he was willing to open his heart and confide in her about the things that mattered to him most, then she would so the same. She must finally let her walls down and invite him in.

"I do," the marquess said slowly, and it seemed to Ellen that he was gearing himself up to tell her something very sensitive.

Ellen waited patiently as they walked, unwilling to push him. Whatever he wished to tell her, she would listen with all her heart. At this point, Ellen was not sure there was anything he could say that would make her think less of him. He was lovely, really lovely, and she had not treated him at all properly. Right from the beginning, she had been cruel, but still he had persisted. Ellen was starting to think the marquess might be a man of whom her father would entirely approve.

CHAPTER 27

ARTHUR DID NOT KNOW what he was doing, if this was the right move to make, but he had no choice now. He had already said too much; he must continue. He also wanted to share this side of his life with Miss Ellen, and he felt it was incredibly important to do so. After all, they had an undeniable connection he had no wish to ignore. Nor did he want to any longer. Not only would it show Miss Ellen more of him and his life and help her understand his character better, it was also vitally linked to what was happening now.

As he dug up his old memories, Arthur's stomach twisted painfully, making his brain feel suddenly cloudy. That was why he tried to avoid going too far back in time; because it was so hard. It really took a toll on him.

"My mother. . ." he rasped, "she is not here any longer. She passed away when I was very young. I was always told it was from a sickness, but I know that is not the truth. I know I have been lied to by my father." Speaking those words aloud left him dizzy. They came more freely than he had thought they would. He could hardly remain standing, he was so affected. But Miss Ellen was staring at him expectantly, waiting to hear more.

"I do not know the details of what exactly she suffered from, but my mother was deemed mad. She had a serious mental affliction which always plagued her." He sniffed hard, trying not to let the sadness bring him to tears. It was a struggle because he had never said any of it to another person before. "To me, my memories of her all involve her seeming particularly tortured and lost. But I did nothing to help her." Miss Ellen gasped and clapped her hand to her mouth in shock. If she was upset her by his reference to madness and, in turn, to her pretense, that was not his intention. He was not trying to make her feel guilty, he simply wanted her to understand.

"I wish I could have done more to help her, Ellen. I look back and I feel absolutely terrible because I did not do more for her. What if I could have saved her? She could still be here now, alive and happy at long last, but she is not."

Ellen squeezed his arm reassuringly. Arthur appreciated her gesture.

"Marquess, may I call you Arthur? "

"Of course. "

"You must know that there was nothing you could have done. You were a child. And even as an adult there is not always something one can do to help. I could not help my father, and I was standing right next to him when he had his heart attack. But I fear that, with a person's mental health, there is even less one can do to assist them."

Arthur thought she could probably say that to him all she wished, but he was still not sure he would ever be able to believe it. He knew he would always going to torture himself and blame his lack of action for his mother not being alive today.

"I wish I could go back in time," he continued instead. "I think about it a lot. I often wish I could go back to change things, to make life better for my mother. Perhaps if she had known the love with which she was surrounded—" His words trailed off. Arthur knew there was no point in talking any more. There was only so much he could say. Nothing could ever change what had happened, or how he felt about it.

"Anyway, that is what I wanted to tell you." He offered her a small shrug, trying to hide the extent of his true feelings. "I thought you should know. I understand what grief can do to a person. Especially someone like you, Ellen, because you have lost both parents. I know it must have been terrible."

Ellen bit down thoughtfully on her bottom lip before she spoke out once more. "May I ask you how your mother died?"

"I have my suspicions," Arthur confessed. "But I cannot be sure. I do not know. My father, I do not get the truth from him; he has done nothing but lie to me. I do not suppose I shall ever get the truth from him, which is very difficult for me."

They walked a little more, but this time they headed back towards the house. But Arthur was not ready to return to the ball just yet. He was not fully convinced that Ellen had been fully truthful with him before, yet again. He hoped that by telling his story, she would finally let him know her true thoughts and feelings.

"So, Ellen, may I ask you again, if you were merely pretending to be mad?" She did not say anything for a long moment, which sent Arthur's heart racing. He could not handle the lying any longer; it was getting too much for him. If Ellen spoke the honest truth to him right now, then he would forgive all.

"I simply have not been feeling like myself recently," she said hesitantly.

His heart sank. She was still not being truthful. "It is my grief; I am sure of it. The stress of losing the man I considered my best friend, the man who took charge of everything. On top of that, I do not believe I have yet recovered from watching him pass away."

Suddenly, Arthur stopped himself from judging her. Perhaps Miss Ellen was telling him the truth, and this really was what she had been suffering. He had no idea how the strain might have affected her. It must have been so difficult for her to face everything head-on, without the patriarch of her household to guide her.

"I am sorry," he said quietly. "I should not have said that. I suppose I am simply worried because, where I could not help my mother, I wish to help you." Miss Ellen hung her head low. She could not seem to meet his eyes. Did that mean she really was being dishonest with him? Because if Arthur thought back over her past behavior, there were times when it seemed as if she should have been able to control her moods and emotions. Especially during the outbursts.

"I do not wish you to apologize," she finally replied. "You have done nothing wrong. I understand that you are simply attempting to be careful. You have been through a lot in your life, and that has shaped you. It makes sense."

Arthur did not know what to make of this statement. Miss Ellen had certainly not given him everything he'd hoped for from their private conversation. He had wanted so desperately to reach a better understanding with her. And he wanted so much to understand her better. But he was still just as confused. Perhaps he needed to simply ask her once and for all how she felt about him. A straight answer would clear up all his concerns. And it would surely be better for them both.

He parted his lips, willing the question to come out of his mouth, but, somehow, he ended up saying nothing at all. It was not as straightforward as it should have been. How could he ask her outright if she really did care for him when the answer might destroy him?

"Do you wish to head back inside?" Miss Ellen asked as soon as they reached the balcony. "Or are you enjoying the moonlight too much?" Arthur could tell that was her way of asking if he needed some more time to collect himself after he had just been so very honest with her. He very much needed that time, but not for the reason she suspected.

"Let us take a little bit of time. Just a few more moments—" Miss Ellen waited patiently beside him, which Arthur appreciated greatly. It was just one of the things he liked about her.

In fact, there were many things he liked about her. If only he could figure out if she was telling him the truth or not. "Ellen, there is actually one more thing I would like to say—" he braved admitting aloud. "If you do not mind me being so bold—" She looked at him warily. Arthur could tell she was concerned he was about to bring up her mental state once more. But since he did not seem to be getting anywhere with that, he decided to take a different tack.

"I do not mind—"

She did not sound certain, but he pushed on. Arthur was certain at that point that he had no choice in the matter. If he did not get around to asking the question, then he would never know. The ball was an important night for them both. He had already decided he must come out of the evening with answers, and this was how he was going to do it.

"Ellen, you said that you did not wish to marry me in the beginning, that you had a poor impression of me, and you did not care much for me." She nodded tentatively, clearly not sure where Arthur was going.

"But your impression of me has changed. So, I suppose, what I wish to know is how you feel about me now?" She sucked in a shocked breath, her eyes flying wide open. Had he been too forward in asking her? Perhaps she was not ready to confess her deepest emotions. But unfortunately, he could not hold back; he absolutely had to know.

One way or another, he had to be sure he was doing the right thing by pursuing her. If she did not want him, even after spending time together alone, then the engagement ball would have all been for nothing. He would have to let his father down. He was going to have to figure out a way to get over the feelings he had developed for Ellen Greenfield.

CHAPTER 28

ELLEN DID NOT like the way she had been continually lying to the marquess, even when assuring him that she was not. But it had gone too far now; she could not admit outright that she had been falsifying everything. He would be too hurt and never want anything to do with her again.

Surprisingly, that was not what she wanted anymore. But that heartbreaking story about his mother had crushed her spirits and made her realize how truly terribly she had been behaving. When Ellen had first come up with the plan to pretend she was mad, she'd believed it to be little more than something from a fairy tale, a story, not something to happen in real life.

She certainly did not know that the poor marquess had been through a genuine case of it himself. If she'd had had any inkling what his mother had experienced, she never would have done it. The last thing she wanted to do was make him feel any worse.

And now here he was, looking her in the eyes and asking her how she really felt about him. This moment was pivotal. Everything could change depending on what she answered next. She could push him away, once and for all, and forget this little tryst had ever happened. She could continue to search for love in her own manner and not worry about Gracelyn's next move.

After all, Ellen stood no chance of stopping her sister if she decided she wished to marry the duke, if he would have her. But Ellen knew with certainty that she did not wish to push the marquess away any longer. As mad as it was, she did not wish to live a life without him in it.

Perhaps things had not happened in the way she'd wished they would, but their union would surely *not* be a loveless marriage of convenience for financial gain. There were real feelings developing between herself and the marquess, and they seemed to grow whenever they were together. It did not help Ellen that he looked so handsome, that his sparkling eyes were a reminder that he was nothing like the foolish, greedy man she had built him up to be in her head.

Ellen had unfairly judged him on sight, and this was the moment she had to truly repent for that, or the marquess might walk away from her forever. The moonlight glittered on his eyes, which glowed as he smiled at her. He did not seem to mind that she was taking some time to formulate her answer. If he was offended, he did not show it. Ellen let her lips fall open, the truth aching to spill from them. Unfortunately, before she could speak, a terrible thought clouded her brain—it was not just the marquess she had to think about, was it?

Much as she wanted to forget the duke existed, because her life was so much better without him in it, she could not. While the marquess might not have an ulterior motive for wanting to marry her, his father definitely did. His father wished to take away her father's land and to do whatever he wanted with it. It might not have been in the best condition now, but who knew what the duke would do to it? The land might never be the same again, and then all memories of her father would be erased.

Ellen simply did not want someone like duke to have the land, possibly disrespecting her father, who was not alive to defend himself. She turned away from the marquess and closed for a moment, so she could think about her wonderful father and what he might tell her to do if he were here. Would he tell her to get Gracelyn and Joy as far away from the duke as possible? Or would he tell her to dive into the pool of feelings which so desperately wanted to swallow her up whole?

Even with her eyes closed, Ellen could not help but notice how acutely aware of the marques she was. He was warm, while the air was cold, and every movement of his prickled her skin, sending delightful electrical shocks darting all through her body. She was not sure she could keep playing the game any longer. She did not know what she was supposed to do next.

Stuck at a crossroads, Ellen struggled to get anywhere near enough air in her body. She was breathless, and her emotions were in w whirl. "Arthur—" she began, turning to look at him at last.

"—The kiss we shared the other day made me realize a lot of things." Ellen could not believe she was confessing this aloud. She so desperately hoped it did not turn out to be a mistake.

"It made me realize that all this time, I have been falling in love with you, which is something I did not expect at all."

Ellen could not stop a smile from spreading across her face. It was nerve-racking and terribly frightening, no doubt about it, but there was something surprisingly liberating about letting out something truly honest.

Now, if she was to say it all, and then the marquess rejected her, she was not sure how she would take it. But, even though she had been trying to repulse him, she had a feeling he would not. After all, he had gone to all this effort to ensure she had the most wonderful ball in the world held in her honor.

Surely he had to feel something for her? She'd felt the same way when they'd kissed as well. She could not believe there was nothing behind it; that simply made no sense.

But the marquess was silent, and there was something truly unnerving about it. It made her very uncomfortable. She did not know what else to do aside from keep talking, trying to explain away her behavior in a way that did not make him hate her for feigning the same affliction that his poor mother had truly suffered from—and which had perhaps ultimately killed her.

"I also loved my father very much," she continued rapidly, her words tripping over one another. "The fields around our estate were his livelihood. He put so much of himself into them. I think that is why I am so passionate about not allowing the land to be used in a way that might disrespect his memory." As she said that, her eyes unexpectedly filled up with tears.

Ellen averted her gaze quickly in the hope that the marquess might not see her tears. "I am attached to the land in the way I was attached to him. We were very close, you see."

I understand that," the marquess replied quietly. "If my father had a different temperament, perhaps I would be closer with him also. I know what it is like to grow up with only one parent. I had no siblings either."

"You must have been so lonely," Ellen sympathized, thinking of Joy. But then she thought of Gracelyn, and she was not so sure siblings were always such a good thing. Perhaps it was easier growing up alone and not having to worry about anyone else.

"I would have liked to be close to someone—" Ellen drowned in her guilt once more. She knew she absolutely must bring up the tricky subject of the 'horse-father', but in a way that did not ruin the closeness that was intensifying between her and Arthur. She was becoming addicted to that feeling.

"I believe that is why, in my mind, my father and the horse have become as one." Ellen tried her best to sound sincere, but she could hardly avoid cringing. "Because of their love for the fields. That is why I struggle to let him go."

The marquess tucked his finger underneath her chin, bringing Ellen's eyes up to meet his. He must have been able to see the tears there, aching to burst free and spill down her cheeks, but he did not pull away in horror.

Instead, he cocked his head to one side and smiled at her softly. She could feel him communicating to her without saying a single word. "Miss Ellen, you do not need to explain yourself to me. I am terribly sorry for even asking you. That was not right. I know better than anyone how crushing grief can be, and how it is easier to cling on to anything of that person, just to keep them in your life a little bit longer. Perhaps that is what I have been doing by torturing myself all this time. It is better to feel bad for not helping my mother when I might have than to forget about her completely. My memories of her are already a little hazy. I want to keep her alive somehow."

Now *that* was something Ellen understood completely. She found it hard to recall her own mother these days. Her flame-red hair was a feature Ellen could never forget, but her features were a little blurry.

Were her eyes blue or green? Did she have a similar frown to Grace-lyn's or Joy's lilting laugh? Ellen was so young when her mother had died, she could hardly blame herself for the memories slipping away. But she felt absolutely certain she would not forget her father. Not when he had been her best friend for such a long time.

"You have not yet returned the favor," she reminded him, trying to change the topic before she really did lose herself to tears. "You have not told me how you feel about me." Arthur smiled widely as he stroked his thumb up and down her cheek. With every movement of his finger, it became increasingly difficult to remain steady and upright. His touch was making her weak at the knees. But she could not fall. Not yet. Not until she had her answer from him once and for all.

CHAPTER 29

"Oh, Ellen," Arthur replied with a happy lilt to his tone. "I would have thought it is quite obvious how I feel about you." She stared back at him blankly. Perhaps he had not been quite as transparent as he'd assumed.

"Miss Ellen, I have been fascinated by you since the very first moment I laid eyes on you. I knew immediately there was something special about you, something which I had never come across before in any woman. It was instantaneous." He smiled widely at her. "You knocked me off my feet. I cannot express to you how monumental that moment was for me."

Miss Ellen looked at him with amazement, her face flushed enchantingly. Arthur became annoyed at himself; perhaps he was not explaining it properly?

"I-t-truly did not know it was possible for anyone to feel that way about me," she stuttered.

That stunned Arthur to the core. He would have thought Miss Ellen would have any number of suitors lining up to court her. Even without the promise of a large dowry, she was so beautiful, any man would be lucky to be with her.

But Arthur was grateful that no one else had ever said these things to her—because he was the one who so desperately wanted to be with her. He could not imagine her married to anyone else. In fact, the idea would absolutely kill him.

"Miss Ellen, the more I have gotten to know you, the more fascinating you become. I love you. In fact, I am head over heels in love with you."

He could not help himself; he dipped his head and pressed his lips gently to hers. It was something he had been wanting to do all night long. Ever since he'd last kissed her, in fact, and the sensation of her plump, luscious lips meeting his was wonderful.

Of course, he was in love with her. He stood no chance around her. She was magnificent, a wonderful woman. Her grief and the way she had reacted to her loss certainly did not put him off. If anything, it endeared her to him even more.

By the time they pulled apart, just a little, Arthur was stunned by the glazed look in Miss Ellen's eyes. She looked las if her feet were barely touching the ground—because she was in heaven. All Arthur wanted to do was spin her around here in the garden and dance with her. It barely even mattered that there was no music playing.

"But your father—" As soon as the words fell out of Miss Ellen's mouth, Arthur instinctively knew what she was worrying about. He was also acutely aware that he was one of the only people in the world who could make things right.

That was a challenge he took seriously. One he intended to complete.

"Ellen—" He held her hands tightly. "I am not interested in any profits that can be made from your fields. That has absolutely nothing to do with the feelings I have for you. In fact, I do not wish to marry you in exchange for the land. I never agreed to that in the first place. If we get married, I would prefer it if you retained the estate. Especially because it makes you so happy. I would not wish you to lose something that means so very much to you. It would not be right. Plus, I truly believe that the estae can become a beautiful place once more. Exactly as it used to be. We can recreate the memories you have—we can make it a place to truly honor the great man your father was."

Miss Ellen squeezed his hands a little tighter. Her eyes flew wide with surprise. "You really mean that? I would not wish for you to have any kind of trouble with your father. I know the land is all he wishes to have—because of the King—"

"I have no interest in pleasing the King," Arthur scoffed. "My only worry is you. I wish very much for you to be happy once more, not be forced to lose something so dear to you. It does not seem fair to me that the estate is up for negotiation at all if it is not something you wish to sell."

Miss Ellen looked as if she was floating on air. It was very clear to Arthur that a weight had been lifted from her shoulders. If only Arthur had known that was all he needed to do. He could have reassured her so much sooner.

She rose to her tiptoes and flung her arms around him tightly. Like a moth to a flame, she did not seem able to resist kissing him even more passionately than last time. Even with the knowledge that kissing a woman at a ball in seclusion was wrong, the temptation was far too powerful for him to resist. He was completely overwhelmed by her. He wished they could remain away from the ball, kissing all night long.

"Oh, Ellen," he whispered as he rested his forehead against hers, to could block out the rest of the world and forget that it even existed, just for a moment. It was only the two of them. "I am very excited for the next stage of our relationship. I am truly excited for our wedding and the love and companionship we shall share afterwards." He stroked the soft skin of her cheek some more. "And I would like you to be sure that you are not mad. You are simply dealing with your grief in the best way you can, and there is nothing wrong with that. Nothing at all."

She rested her hand on top of his. "You truly feel that way?"

He chuckled lightly. "Of course, I do. I understand what a terrible experience you have had. I see *you* now. Really see you. I truly hope you see me too."

"I do," she reassured him. "I really do. I see you, and I love what I see. Thank you so much for confiding in me. It means everything. I love getting to know the real you."

"Me too." He nodded and smiled. "I love you so very much."

They remained exactly where they were, though Arthur was not sure for how long. It was impossible to know how fast time was ticking by, and he did not care. This was the only place in the world he wanted to be. It was a little bubble, and only the two of them were inside it. Everyone else had been completely blocked out.

But they could not remain there for too long, simply looking at one another. Not with the intense chemical pull between them that was impossible to ignore. It was irresistible: they were drawn back together. They had no choice but to kiss some more. Arthur was so happy to know that once they were married, this would happen all the time. They could exist in their own little world, where he knew they would both be so very happy. Ellen brought him a joy he knew would sustain him forever, and he hoped he could do the same for her. That was all he wanted.

Yes, it was going to create friction between himself and his father, he knew that much. The duke would be very unhappy about losing the Greenfield land and the King's approval, but Arthur still felt it was the right thing to do.

"I suppose we are going to have to go back inside eventually," Arthur chuckled, but he was unable to hide his regret. "Since we are the main attraction at the ball, our presence shall be missed. The last thing we want is for people to come searching for us. We do not wish to draw attention to ourselves."

He did not say it aloud, but he knew that if people came searching for them, and they found them in this state, they would be the gossip of society for months. The duke would never forgive him if he brought shame on the family and ruined their reputation.

Plus, he had gotten everything he'd wanted—and more. He'd thrown the engagement ball to allow Miss Ellen to see just how much he adored her, and now he had managed to say so with words. Everything was so much better.

He loved Miss Ellen, and she loved him too. They could overcome anything else.

They walked back inside the ball, to find everyone dancing and enjoying themselves just as much as they had been before they'd gone outside. No one seemed to notice they had been gone, thank goodness. They simply continued with their night as if nothing had happened. But that was not the case for Arthur. His whole world had been turned upside down—in the best way possible.

Their worlds remained exactly what they once were, and it was a unique experience.

Nothing could get in their way now. Nothing could ruin this wonderful mood. Arthur had finally found his happiness, something he never could have imagined when he first went on that trip with his father to the Greenfield estate. He was unhappy then, displeased by the necessity for the journey. Little had he guessed he was going to find everything that day which he did not even know he was searching for.

But love could come from the strangest of places, and Arthur was happy. Having the most beautiful woman he had ever laid eyes on holding on to his arm, celebrating their engagement and knowing it was something they both wanted— It was amazing! Arthur could not stop himself from grinning ear to ear. He was floating on air and looking forward to the rest of the night.

CHAPTER 30

Arthur's positive mood did not subside all night long, despite not getting much sleep. Though his body was weary after the excitement of the engagement ball, his brain was in a spin all night long. He could not stop thinking about the beautiful Ellen, planning their marriage, and thinking about what their life together would be like. Arthur knew he would be happy forever.

So, as he descended the stairs that morning, heading towards the dining room, where his father was already seated eating his breakfast, Arthur was on top of the world. He could not imagine the duke had anything to say to bring his mood down.

Before Arthur could even take a seat, the maid had his breakfast sitting in front of him. He did not even have to think about what he had to eat. He'd never had to; it had always been the same way. For a moment, though, he could not help but wonder what things were like for Miss Ellen and her sisters. Perhaps once upon a time, they'd had people to work for their family, but no longer.

Poor Ellen, as the eldest sister, had so much strain on her shoulders. It had to be a very hard life; no wonder the grief was especially difficult for her to manage. Arthur knew he could not blame her for a single thing. He would spend the rest of his life talking to the "horse-father" if that was what she wished.

"Well, Arthur, that was a very interesting ball last night," his father began with a knowing tone. Arthur was immediately wary. There was something in his father's voice that put him on edge. "I am very glad you decided to hold it."

"You are?" His father had shown absolutely no interest in the engagement ball before it had happened. In fact, he had actively been against it because he did not believe in the upcoming marriage. "I did not know you would enjoy it so much."

"Mmm, yes, it was rather good." Theduke nodded his head slowly. A smirk curled up onto his lips, which made Arthur's heart race a whole lot faster. "I had a very good time. Getting to know the young Miss Gracelyn was very inspiring."

Arthur's heart sank. He did not like the glint in his father's eye one bit. He shifted uncomfortably in his seat, almost forgetting about his breakfast in the process. He had been so happy only moments ago, he did not think it possible to change that. But in one fell swoop, his father had well and truly managed it.

"I did not know you had spent so much time with Miss Gracelyn."

Of course, Arthur had seen it. He did not like it last night at the ball, but he had been far too distracted by the stunning Ellen and her final confession of her love for him, so he had not worried about it much as he should have done.

But now it was all he could worry about.

"Oh, yes, she is rather enthralling." That was the highest praise Arthur had heard his father give any woman. It stripped the air from his lungs. "I find her fascinating, and last night, I was able to see her in a new light. Of course, she would have looked much more appealing in a finer gown, but that can be changed."

"Can be changed? How?" Arthur's breaths began to ball up in his throat. They were not even reaching his lungs anymore, which left him a little dizzy.

"Well, I am sure that, one day, she will find a husband who can financially provide for her, to ensure she shines at every ball."

Arthur gasped and slid back in his chair slightly. The duke had not mentioned himself as a potential suitor in that scenario. He didn't have to; the glint in his eyes spoke volumes. It had been mentioned in passing that if Arthur did not marry Miss Ellen then he would take another one of the Greenfield sisters to wed, but he had not taken that seriously. He did not think his father would really want to marry such a young girl.

"Any man would be lucky to be her husband," the duke continued, as if oblivious to Arthur's inner turmoil. "I have to admit that Miss Gracelyn is the most beautiful woman I have ever seen. Plus, she has a wit like no other."

He stared off into the distance, evidently in a daydream about Miss Gracelyn. It was deeply disturbing to Arthur; he had never seen anything like it on his father's face before. It was horrible. He did not know what to say.

Arthur actually found his mouth moving before his brain had caught up, so he did not think about what he was saying. "Father, did my mother mean nothing to you? How can you say such things about Miss Gracelyn, as if Mother meant nothing at all?"

The duke's expression did not change at all. It did not seem to matter that Arthur was upset about his mother. That smirking smile remained on his face.

"Your mother was the—erm —the perfect woman," he replied with a sense of biting humor behind his words. "Just not the perfect woman for *me*."

Arthur was completely taken aback. The duke's dark chuckle sent chills racing down his spine. Just because the words had been spoken quietly, it did not make them hurt any less. In that terrible moment, Arthur became acutely aware that his father had never truly loved his mother. She had meant nothing to him. Perhaps he had married her for convenience, to benefit his own family financially, and it never became anything more than that. He had never cared for her at all.

That was terribly sad. Arthur's heart broke; he felt so deeply for his mother. He hoped she had not passed away thinking that no one loved her. He actually had to hold on to his chest for a moment, asif to prevent his heart from shattering into a million pieces.

"I cannot believe that you actually said that," he finally rasped. "No wonder Mother struggled so much. You did not love her as a husband should."

The duke rolled his eyes, apparently untroubled by Arthur's words, even though they had been supposed to have a serious impact on him. "You know nothing about my marriage to your mother. You also know nothing about her sickness. Nothing could have been done to save her."

"You have lied to me forever." Arthur rose to his feet, his heart pounding in his chest. "You have always told me that it was a physical sickness that killed her, but I know that is not the truth. I know she struggled with her mental state—"

"Does it matter now?" the duke sneered. "I do not see how it makes any difference. Whether she died through a physical illness or something else."

"It matters to me." Arthur began to struggle to keep his tone under control. The last thing he wanted to do was yell at his father because that was a fight he would never win. What he needed to do was stay rational, so that he could say everything he needed to get out. And much as he wanted to keep attacking the duke about his mother, there was something else too. "But if we are going to speak of love, and marriage, then there is something I want to tell you."

The duke turned away from Arthur and continued to sip his tea as if his son was not talking at all. But that would not stop Arthur.

"After speaking with Miss Ellen at the ball last night, I have realized the value the land around the estate has to the Greenfield family. I do not wish to take it from them."

He braced himself, waiting for his father to yell, but the duke did not take that approach. Instead, he laughed. "Oh dear, it is happening. You are being manipulated by the girl. She is using her feminine charms to get what she wants from you."

"That is not like Miss Ellen at all," Arthur argued, incensed. "She is not doing that. The feelings we have for one another are genuine. As are her feelings for the pastures. You might not understand that, but her father put so much love into that land. The Greenfield sisters deserve to keep a piece of him alive."

"The fields might have been something to commemorate a long time ago, but they are dead now." The duke shrugged. Nothing bothered him one bit. "They can commemorate their fields when I have it producing plenty of barley for the King."

"That will not be happening." Arthur shook his head. "You will not be using the Greenfield land to grow barley. If you wish to continue your deal with the king, you shall have to find another solution."

Arthur did not wait around for his father to reply. He did not want to hear his response because it would not be rational. At least he now knew where Arthur stood, though, and hopefully, the duke would accept it and move on with another plan.

Miss Ellen was going to keep her land, no matter what happened.

Arthur was going to make sure of that. No matter what it took, no matter how many fights he was forced to have with his father, he would make sure she kept her estate. It would become a glorious place where she could get over her grief much more effectively.

Arthur would never become the sort of husband his father had been. Never.

CHAPTER 31

OF COURSE, Arthur was not going to get away from his father. He probably should have not bothered walking away because if the duke wanted to say something, he would make sure it was heard, whether the other person wanted to hear it or not. It was mere seconds before the duke began to shout.

"I cannot believe you would risk everything," he shouted, stopping Arthur in his tracks. He sighed heavily and paused. There was no point in running any longer. "That was the plan all along. We would not have even approached the Greenfield girls if it were not for the land. If I was to choose a wife for you under other circumstances, I would have chosen one with more to offer."

Arthur pressed his lips together tightly, so he did not explode. It was getting increasingly hard to keep his temper. "I am happy with Miss Ellen Greenfield. I do not have any issues with the decisions made. I am simply stating that I will not marry her so that you can have the land. That is not how it will be."

The duke Edward let out a frustrated growl. "Why are you behaving in this manner? You will not change my mind. You will not wed any of the Greenfield girls if I cannot have the land because then, there would be no benefit at all. Arthur, you are not even thinking about the potential profits this agreement with the King will bring. I thought you were interested in being involved in the business."

"I do not know how you got that impression."

Arthur might have been acting rather childishly now, but he could not seem to get on the same level as his father, no matter how hard he tried.

"Think of future business endeavors, Arthur," his father continued. "If we back out of this now, and the arrangement with the King falls through, can you please think about how that will affect the Maxwell name? Our reputations will be ruined. No one of any status will wish to deal with us again. Can you understand what that will do to us?"

In a way, that affected Arthur more than he had thought possible. He might not have been interested in the barley business or working alongside his father, but he did not like the idea of the Maxwell name being tarnished.

But at the same time, was it worth breaking Miss Ellen's heart just to keep his father happy? Just to ensure that the duke could continue to make huge profits his barley business and please the King? Arthur knew his father would become absolutely unbearable once he had the King on his side. His head would inflate, and he would become impossible to live with.

"I can see you do not understand a thing." The duke threw his hands in the air in frustration. "I do not know what else I can say to you. I do not know how to make you see the damage you are doing by behaving like this. This is terrible."

Arthur knew he should reply, but he did not have any words. He had said everything he wished to say; there was nothing else. His point had been made, and his father had disagreed with it. Until one of them gave way, that was it. Arthur knew it was not going to be him.

The duke finally gave in and stormed off to his study, slamming the door so hard behind him, the sound echoed through the whole building. Perhaps that should have been the end of it. Maybe Arthur should have taken the opportunity to steal off to his room, so there could be no more yelling, but something deep in his gut warned him otherwise. He felt he should follow his father, just in case.

Arthur was incredibly nervous as he stepped quietly through the hallways of his home. He followed his father to the study and pressed himself up against the door to listen in. He thought his father might be making plans, making calculations that Arthur needed to be aware of. But he did not hear a thing. That did not stop him from worrying that nefarious behavior might be afoot.

Arthur pulled himself away from the door, his head spinning, and he moved backwards. He must figure out what was going on, but he did not want his father to become suspicious of him.

"What do I do?" Arthur asked himself quietly as he walked away, chewing on his thumbnail. He had to do something.

His mind kept darting to one place only; to Ellen. To the Greenfield girls. If his father was going to do anything, he would not attack his own son. Not directly. He was too concerned with the Maxwell name and its reputation. No, if he was going to do anything to get his own way, he would attack the women.

Arthur took a step towards the front door, considering grabbing his coat and heading straight to Ellen's home, so he could at least warn her to be on the alert. Mentally, he already had a carriage ready to take him to the Greenfield estate. He was almost out the front door before he suddenly stopped in his tracks.

Wait, no. That was not the best move. Arthur prevented himself from leaving, allowing himself to think before he acted. His pulse was pounding wildly, almost out of control, which was not a good sign.

The first time Arthur had gone to the Greenfield home without his father's knowledge, the duke had followed him and created a scene. He had been very careful since then to ensure his father had absolutely no idea what was going on, which was exactly why he could not go there just now. Arthur knew his father was going to be expecting that.

It was absolutely the worst thing he could do, so as much as it might kill him to have to wait, it was better for Ellen and her sisters. The last thing Arthur wanted was for his father to become vindictive toward the woman he himself loved.

But impatience was already creeping through his veins, threatening to kill him, like a slow, deadly illness. The only thing Arthur could do was to keep reassuring himself that it was best for the Greenfield girls.

Eventually, Arthur took himself back to the breakfast table. He might not have had any intention of eating because his father had well and truly destroyed his appetite, but because he needed to sit still for a moment.

If he did not remain fixed to one place, he might not need a carriage. He might run to the Greenfield estate just because he so desperately wanted to hold Ellen, to reassure her that all would be well.

Arthur had woken up feeling so happy; he had not thought anything could bring down his mood. But his father had destroyed everything. All

Arthur wanted was to get married to this beautiful woman, to ensure she kept the land that made her so happy, and to have their happily ever after.

If only he had another family, a normal family, where he would be allowed to do whatever he wished. Maybe if his mother was alive, then things would be different. She would likely be on his side. She would want him to be happy, especially since it seemed she had been so unhappy in her own marriage—stuck with a man who cared nothing for her, who called the young Miss Gracelyn the most beautiful woman he had ever laid eyes on. A statement that would haunt Arthur forever.

Arthur leaned his head forward on the table and allowed it to fall hard against the mahogany wood as a strong sense of helplessness overcame him. It hurt him so much to think that his mother, who had already been suffering from a mental illness, had also had to suffer a loveless marriage with his father. He could only imagine that it had only aggravated her condition, making her increasingly unhappy with every passing moment.

And now his father was talking about Miss Gracelyn as if he was going to marry her. Arthur would not let that happen, but it was even more worrying to assume that he would now pursue that plan aggressively to get his hands on the Greenfield land. To make sure his deal with the King went through.

That was just about the only thing he cared about.

"I cannot let that happen," Arthur whispered desperately under his breath. "I do not know what my plan is, but I will not allow him anywhere near her."

Time passed, Arthur was not sure how much, but it seemed a lot. His father had not come out of his study for what seemed like hours. It left Arthur feeling rather lost. In the end, the only thing he could do was head upstairs to his chambers, to stew over his worries and thoughts for the rest of the day.

It was going to be a long day, as he was going to be listening out for his father the entire time.

CHAPTER 32

THE BLOODCURDLING SCREAM SOUNDED INHUMAN. Ellen looked about, alarmed. It seemed to be coming from everywhere but nowhere at the same time. It was only when she noticed her chest vibrating that she realized the sound was coming from within her.

It was shocking, the cry of a banshee perhaps? Ellen knotted her fingers in her hair as she wailed out her pain. She wanted nothing more than to wake up and find it was all a terrible nightmare.

It could not be real. She could not accept it. It was too much to handle. But she was not waking up, and that scream was loud enough to wake a sleeping drunk. It must be real!

"Ellen!" Joy screamed as she raced across the fields to reach her sister. Had Ellen's screams been so loud that she could be heard in the house? "Ellen, what is it?"

Even Gracelyn was racing toward her, still in her nightgown because it was so early in the morning. It was the time of day where the sun had just risen and the orange light was weak, contrasting against the beautiful blue of the landscape. She might not have been yelling out to Ellen to see if she was all right, as Joy was, but there was definite concern in her expression, which was shocking. Gracelyn had not cared about Ellen for a while.

But even that wasn't enough to make Ellen stop screaming. She just could not seem to stop. She did not have a connection between her mouth and her brain anymore. The horrible shock of the moment was too much for her to bear.

"What is the matter?" Joy wrapped her arms tightly around Ellen, reminding her that was connected to the real world. "What is wrong?"

"The—the —" Ellen so desperately wanted to explain, so her sisters could understand what her pain was all about, but she could not get the words out. Her brain was shaking, her body trembling, the whole world had fallen out from underneath her feet. Her breathless lungs could not form sounds.

"Oh, my goodness," Gracelyn burst out as she arrived. "The horse. It's the horse, isn't it? The horse is missing?"

Hearing Gracelyn say it brought Ellen to her knees. Now it was confirmed—her horse had gone. She was not dreaming; it was really happening, the horse who had brought her endless comfort, even if she knew he was not really her father, was gone. What was she going to do now? She could not even begin to imagine recovering from his loss. Her life would not be the same without her horse.

"What has happened?" Joy demanded, as alarmed as Ellen. "Could he have run away? Was there a storm last night or something that could have spooked him? But then, how would he have gotten out of the stable?"

"It is always locked up," Gracelyn confirmed. "So, I do not think so—"

Ellen had to agree. "Our horse has never run off before. Ever. He has been out here when there have been loud noises and storms, and it has never affected him. I do not understand."

"Then what could have happened?" Joy asked helplessly, throwing her hands in the air in frustration. "It does not make any sense."

Ellen folded her arms across her chest as the tears ran down her face. "I know what has happened," she growled angrily. "I know exactly what has happened. Our horse has been stolen, and I know by whom."

Joy and Gracelyn both stared at Ellen with wide, shocked eyes. Neither of them said a word as they waited for her to continue. She sucked in a deep, shaky breath before she spoke. What she was about to say was dangerous. But it had to be said.

"The duke," she said. "He is behind this. He has done this to punish me."

Joy paled. All the color drained from her cheeks. Gracelyn had a different reaction though. Her cheeks burned brightly, and her eyes flashed with rage.

"What are you talking about?" Gracelyn snapped defensively. "Why on earth would you suspect the duke? I am sure he has his own horses. He has enough money to purchase plenty of horses. Why should he steal ours?"

Ellen shook her head. "This has nothing to do with money. This is punishment, as I said. I spoke to the marquess at our engagement ball and told him that I would not like to give up our father's fields. Not even for marriage. I told him all about my love for the fields, our love for the fields —" She extended her arms wide to try and include her sisters, but Gracelyn was far too angry for that. "The marquess feels compassion for us. He lost his own mother, so he understands what grief is like. He told me he would like to negotiate a deal with his father so that we can keep the land. He wants that for us."

Gracelyn let out a horrified gurgling sound. She did not look impressed by Ellen's statement at all. There was almost a glare of horror in her eyes.

"But the duke wants the land to expand his barley production," Gracelyn replied. "That way, he will have an alliance with the King. We do not wish to get in the way of something so important, surely? Something to bring the Maxwell family so much good fortune. That would be terrible, Ellen."

Anger bubbled up inside Ellen. She curled her fists to attempt to stop herself from leaping on Gracelyn. She had to show her sister how upset she was. "Is that all you are interested in, Gracelyn? Money? Money for the Maxwell family? What about our father? What about his memory? What about this estate being the only home we have ever known?"

Ellen's tears thickened and grew more powerful. Gracelyn was being so callous, so thoughtless about their home. It was almost as if the middle Greenfield sister did not want to hold on to any of their family memories. She could not wait to escape, and probably, when she did, she would never talk to her sisters again.

It was heartbreaking. It left Ellen bending double in agony. She could feel everything about the life she had lived slipping through her fingers. Ellen was not sure that even the marquess would be able to negotiate anything if the duke was intent on marrying Gracelyn anyway. Ellen might not be able to do anything, and now she did not even have her horse anymore. What had happened to her horse? Was she ever going to be able to get him back?

"I can hear a horse right now," Joy gasped, hope flooding her expression. "Do you think it might all be a simple mistake? The horse might be down in the bottom meadow."

Ellen allowed hope to bloom in her chest. Much as she knew she had already caused even more of a rift between herself and Gracelyn, she hoped she was wrong and her horse was still there, on the Greenfield estate. Having the horse back was the most important thing to her just then.

But all the girls very quickly realized that was not the case. There was not just a horse, there was a carriage as well. A visitor! But the girls were not prepared to receive guests, whoever they were. Ellen had bright red eyes from sobbing, Gracelyn was still in her nightgown, and poor Joy looked too shocked to deal with anyone. All the Greenfield girls looked as if they wanted to run inside and to hide from everyone, especially these unknown visitors.

But, of course, they were going to have to greet their guests because that was the polite thing to do. The girls walked slowly towards the carriage, until someone descended.

"Arthur!" Ellen gasped in happy shock. "It is you."

He was about the only person in the world she wanted to see just then. Relief flooded her as she ran toward him. Not only would he make her feel a little better about the missing horse, he might be able to give her answers. If his father had done something to her horse, the marquess might know about it. That was likely why he was here; to help them with the mess created by his father.

Joy also looked happy to see him, clearly relieved to have the marquess there to help them, but Gracelyn did not look pleased at all. She had her hands folded tightly across her chest and her lips pressed together tightly. But Ellen did not care; this was much better than the duke arriving. Now *that* would have been absolutely terrifying for all of them, even if Gracelyn thought she had some connection with him.

She did not. He was a terrible man, and Ellen was convinced he had stolen her horse. With the marquess there, she knew she was going to be able to prove it as well. Gracelyn would have to see the truth now.

CHAPTER 33

As ELLEN NEARED ARTHUR, she felt lighter in her steps. He was a light in the darkness; he had strengthened the sun rays. She ran to him. As the marquess looked up and caught her eye, he broke out into a smile but only for a second. Ellen watched as recognition flickered across his face; he sensed something awful had happened.

Perhaps it was Ellen's red face, still soaking wet with tears. Or the worry evident in Joy's expression. Or maybe the marquess was worried about Gracelyn being outside in her nightgown. Either way, he looked very worried about the Greenfield girls.

"What has happened?" he asked the moment Ellen was within listening distance.

"It is my horse." She hoped he would understand how serious the matter was to her. "He is gone."

The marquess's eyes scanned the fields rapidly as he tried to locate the horse. It took him a couple of moments to fully understand what she had said.

"No, he is gone," she insisted. "He is not here. The stables are empty."

The marquess's eyes flew wide with shock before he groaned. "Oh no, this can't be happening. My father has not sunk so low, has he?"

Ellen could hardly catch her breath. The marquess agreed with her, and she had not even expressed her theory yet. He knew just as well as she did that the duke was behind this. Although, it still stunned her to find she was right. Thinking it and having it confirmed were two very different things.

"How can you say that?" Gracelyn insisted loudly, letting some of her anger out. "How can you jump to that conclusion with no evidence? You must be jealous of your father, that is all I can think of. There is no other reason for you to say such a dreadful thing." She was angry because of her previous argument with Ellen, but, of course, the marquess did not know that. He could not understand what was going on. "You are jealous of him because he is a duke, he is a powerful and well-liked man who is very successful in business. You could never live up to his reputation."

Ellen wanted to jump in and defend Arthur, but she did not need to. He was more than capable of standing up for himself.

"I have absolutely no reason to be jealous of my father," he told her calmly. "That has nothing to do with the horse."

"Your father would never stoop so low as to steal a horse from a failing estate."

A guttural flew out of Ellen's mouth. She knew her sister didn't care about the land, but for her to state so blatantly to another person that they lived on a 'failing estate' was just dreadful.

The marquess shot Ellen a sympathetic look. Even if Gracelyn did not understand the magnitude of what she had just said, he did.

"If there is no horse, no work can be done," he reminded Gracelyn. "Which will cause your estate to fail further. Then you will have no choice but to sell it."

Gracelyn scoffed and rolled her eyes. "You are jumping to conclusions. That horse is old and stupid, who knows what might have happened to him? The one thing I can be sure of is that the duke had nothing to do with it. You should stop saying it because it makes you sound so very silly."

Ellen could hardly stand to look at her middle sister. She caught Joy's eye, but their poor youngest sister seemed trapped in the middle, as if she did not know what to do. All she really wanted to do was to have her sisters be friends once more.

Ellen turned away from Gracelyn and looked to the marquess instead. He was figuring everything out in the same way as she had, and, on top of that, he genuinely cared for the pain she was going through.

Ellen now knew for sure she had been foolish to ever think that the marquess was cold and greedy like his father. He was actually the most compassionate human being she had ever met. No wonder she had fallen in love with him.

Tearfully, she asked him for help. "I need my father back, Marquess of

York. I need the horse to be returned to me. I can't lose him twice. I simply can't."

She knew what she was now stating in front of her sisters, which was dangerous because they might seize on it and demand to know more. Thankfully, Gracelyn was too busy hissing at Joy, trying to get her on her side. Ellen did not think Joy would give in; she would not want to give up the land for barley production, not unless Gracelyn convinced her of the financial benefits.

Ellen swallowed hard. She could not lose Joy. If both her sisters turned on her, then her argument would lose its strength. Ellen did not want to cry in front of the marquess, especially since she was already red-faced, but it was almost impossible to prevent her emotions from overwhelming her. She was crying all over again.

The marquess put his arm around Ellen to comfort her. The warmth of his body did comfort her somewhat, but it was not enough. She was distracted by her worries and fears. If she lost her sisters, then Ellen would be the more alone that she had ever been in her life. She was so full of sorrow, she felt almost deranged.

"I will find out more details," Arthur assured her. "I will go home and find out what is going on. Obviously, as you stated, Miss Gracelyn, I can't be certain that my father has had the horse removed. I do not have evidence of that. But I do have a strong suspicion he is behind it."

"Pft, you think you can outsmart your father?" Gracelyn sneered.

"I think my father is a very persuasive man," Arthur agreed. "So, it will not be easy to prove it, but I will find out the truth."

"I do not think you can do it." Gracelyn shrugged derisively. "And I do not believe you even want to. You know you will make a fool out of your-self. Your father will hate you."

Ellen sucked in a sharp breath and took a step back. She watched in horror as Gracelyn rolled her shoulders back and jutted her chin out in sheer determination. She was not going to back down, no matter what Arthur said. He did not look a if he wanted to back down to Gracelyn either. He was likely very upset with the way his father had been acting toward Gracelyn, just as Ellen was herself.

"I have been living with my father for my entire life," the marquess said calmly. "I know him far better than anyone else. You nnedn't worry about that."

"Humph, that is not what I have heard."

Now Ellen was intrigued. She wished to know what the duke had said to her sister about Arthur, but she could not bring herself to ask. It seemed Arthur did not wish to hear what his father had said about him either.

If the duke really was as cold as Ellen knew him to be, then Arthur had probably been hearing criticisms about himself for his entire life. The duke would doubtless have been chipping away at his son's self-confidence since his birth.

The thought broke Ellen's heart just a little.

Ellen could not cope with the situation any longer. She did not like the argument between her sister and the marquess. It was not helping anything when her horse was still missing. As she blocked her ears to stop the sound from reaching her ears and shut her eyes, it was the image of the horse that flooded her mind. Everyone else might have forgotten her horse was missing, but she had not.

"I need my horse," she wailedShe was reacting badly, in a way that was completely out of her control. "I need my horse here, now!"

It was only when Joy rested her hand on Ellen's shoulder that she snapped out of her wailing. She stared wildly at everyone in turn before she finally snapped. The words came flying out before she could stop them.

"If my horse is not found, there will be no marriage."

Almost as soon she'd said it, Ellen regretted it. It was not the marquess she was upset with. It was his father, and Gracelyn as well. She simply felt trapped in a corner, and she had to attack because there was no other way out. She had to stop everyone from shouting and focusing on all the wrong things. The marquess was guilty of that, she supposed, but only because he cared about her so much. He was on her side, which she appreciated, but now they all had to act!

Ellen had to stop the duke from doing something dreadful to her horse, and she would do whatever it took to stop him.

CHAPTER 34

"THERE SHOULD BE NO WEDDING," Gracelyn shrieked. "Not between the two of you, at least. I can't believe you are even thinking about getting married. Not anymore. You know you do not need to any longer."

Ellen held up her hands to stop her sister from speaking. The last thing she wanted to hear was Gracelyn bleating on about how she was going to marry the duke and give him the estate, no matter what happened with Ellen and Arthur. Ellen could only cope with one problem at a time.

"Maybe you all think I'm simply drowning in grief and self-pity," Ellen shouted, "but something has happened to my horse, and I must find him. I can't lose anyone else. Not now. I simply can't!"

"I have already assured you that I will speak with my father about it," Arthur assured her, but the words did not sink in. She drowning in emotion.

"I know you have said that, but now you are shouting too."

"Because he does not intend to do anything," Gracelyn interjected. "He is not this wonderful fairy tale man you are now pretending he is, who you didn't even like before. Joy and I were the ones who had to talk you into marrying the marquess. Or is that something we are not acknowledging now?"

Ellen darted her eyes anxiously over to Arthur to see how affected he was by those words. Even though he had suspected as much, hearing it come out of her sister's mouth must be really painful for him.

"How is this helpful?" Ellen hissed at her sister. "Stop it."

"I just can't see why you still want him." Gracelyn shrugged. "You know I am on very good terms with the duke now. Everything is taken care of. You do not need to worry about him anymore."

"But my horse—" Ellen said hopelessly as she pointed back towards the stables.

Gracelyn rolled her eyes, acting like the oldest sister, with all the wisdom and knowledge of someone who had a lot of life experience.

"He will not help you with the horse, Ellen. He 'thinks' his father might have taken the horse, but he is not sure. He has also shown that he is far too afraid to stand up to the duke, even if is certain our horse had been stolen."

Deep down, Ellen knew her sister was just trying to get under her skin and upset her, but she could not stop herself from being affected by her words. She might have spent her whole life trying not to be manipulated by Gracelyn, but the terrible day she was experiencing, plus the surge of emotions racing through her, made it harder for Ellen to deal with her.

"Gracelyn, please—" Ellen whispered meekly. She so desperately wanted to put an end to this, but she could not. She was too weak.

"Just admit it, Ellen," Gracelyn snapped back. "You do not trust the marquess at all. You have made it very obvious that you do not trust the duke, so it must annoy you that the marquess will not outright admit that his father has had the horse stolen."

Ellen's head was spinning. Gracelyn was the one who kept pushing the fact that there was no evidence, so why was she suddenly saying that? It was all so confusing. She knew she must say something, anything. She should have defended the marquess in the same way that he had stuck up for her, but for some reason, she could not. Her mouth had gone dry.

"Wait!" The marquess clearly did not have the same problem. He stepped back into the conversation with ease. "I understand that I have not said anything outright, but I have admitted that my father is likely involved. I have also said that I will find out. I do not want to settle fully on my decision without evidence."

Gracelyn smirked and folded her arms across her chest with obvious delight. "You can't love my sister that much then. You cannot be dedicated to marrying her. No wonder she does not trust you."

"I have known my father for my entire life. I have known you for a short while."

Arthur's cheeks burned with anger. Ellen could not help herself; she stepped away from him in shock. She really could not fathom what was going on, but she was very certain this was not a side of the marquess that she had seen before.

"You are all being very unfair," he continued. "Expecting me to immediately dismiss my father. Is that what you think as well, Miss Ellen?"

He stared at her with such burning eyes that Ellen automatically stepped back. She was on the verge of running, which she knew would not help matters. Deep down, she knew that if she took off, the argument between Arthur and Gracelyn would likely get much worse.

"I-I —" She tried really hard, but she could not land on anything else.

"I thought you were better than that, Miss Ellen." The marquess was evidently hurt. It was his turn to start backing away. "I thought you were intelligent and thoughtful. I hardly believe you are in agreement with Miss Gracelyn about this. I am here to help you, and I have not said that my father is innocent, just that I need evidence."

"I—" Ellen gulped, unable to get her words out. This was horrible. She felt trapped inside her own body, unable to react as she wanted. She wanted the whole situation to come to an end now.

"This is terrible," the marquess tutted and shook his head. "I am horrified."

Tears surged down Ellen's cheeks. She still regretted what she had initially said to the marquess, but now he had said some dreadful things to her as well, making her even more confused.

"Then why did you say all those things to me out on the balcony at the ball?" she managed. "If you truly believe I am unintelligent and not at all thoughtful? Perhaps my sister is right." This was the first time Ellen had agreed with Gracelyn in years, but it felt right. "Maybe you are in on your father's plan, and I have been played for fool this entire time. The duke is ruthless; clearly, he will do absolutely anything to get his hands on our land, whether it involves my sister, or you and me. I do not even know what to think anymore."

Ellen broke off from her rant, breathless and dizzy. A thick silence hung in the air. Ellen was sure she'd said far too much, and she had said some things that there was no way of taking back.

The marquess turned his eyes away from Ellen. It was as if he could not stand to even look at her anymore, but she was sure she saw a tear shining in his eye. That shattered her heart into a million pieces. She' felt she had found the true love she had always been looking for, and now she had ruined it, with just a few harsh words. Ellen had pushed him away, possibly for good.

That was why she did not usually agree with anything Gracelyn said. She seldom understood where her middle sister operated, and this was the first time she had agreed with her. But was she right to do so?

Deep down, Ellen knew it was very unlikely that Arthur could be involved in some plot with his father, or he would not have been so kind and compassionate toward her. Ellen was sure the nice side of him was the truth. If the duke had arranged to remove their horse, then he had acted alone.

But she could not make that clear to Arthur now, could she? Because the words she had spoken were out there between them, and she was unable to take them back. Just as Arthur could not take back what he had said to her. Those harsh words.

He thought she was unintelligent.

He thought she was thoughtless.

He had said so himself. Those words had come out of his mouth. She might have been in shock, but Ellen was sure they would stick with her forever.

Maybe the fairy tale romance she thought she'd found, even if it had not begun in the romantic way she'd dreamed of, was not going to work out after all. She might have even inflated it in her mind, to allow herself believe things were better than they really were.

Not only had Ellen lost her father recently, and her horse as well, plus her sisters—now, Arthur Maxwell was going too. She really was completely on her own.

CHAPTER 35

ARTHUR STEPPED BACK IN SHOCK. He could not believe what Miss Ellen had just said. He knew this was a terrible situation, but he could not stop the hurt from circulating through his body. The fact she did not trust him was terrible.

"I think we should go and take a look at the other end of the field," Miss Gracelyn declared loudly, clearly trying to break through the awkwardness surrounding them all. "Come with me, Joy. I can't do it alone."

Joy could not get away from him and Miss Ellen quickly enough. Arthur watched the two women run as if chased by bees. Arthur almost wished he could run off with them so he did not have to face Ellen.

Miss Ellen looked as if she wanted to run as well. Arthur almost wanted to tell her to go so he did not have to deal with her anymore, but he could not. He was not going to leave her without making it very clear that he was never going to be anything like his father.

Arthur parted his lips, about to explain his feelings, but no words came out. A thick ball of emotion lodged in his throat. He could not seem to get any sound past it. He was not even sure who the woman standing before him was.

She did not look like the woman he had been talking to at the ball.

"I have nothing to do with this," he finally managed to blurt out. His voice was trembling as badly as his body was shaking. "Nothing. I can't believe you could think that about me for a moment. I thought I have shown you by now that I am not that person. I would never wish to hurt you, ever."

Miss Ellen's face fell, but Arthur's anger did not allow him to falter. He could not. Not when she was balancing the idea of a potential wedding on this horse. Even if his father was involved in the situation, it was not he, Arthur, who had hurt her.

"I thought that you were an intelligent woman, Ellen," he declared in a shaky tone. "I have thought so very highly of you, but today I am stunned to the core. The way you have behaved—" He tutted to himself and shook his head. "You have acted like a bully."

"I have not—" Miss Ellen started, but Arthur held up his hand to stop her.

"No, I do not wish you to say anything else," he insisted. "I believe you have said more than enough. You do not wish to marry me unless the horse is found. I very much understand." He did not express his own feelings on the potential marriage any longer. He had absolutely no idea how he felt about it. "I will prove to you that I had nothing to do with the disappearance of the horse, though. I will make you see that I am nothing like my father. I never have been, and I never will be."

Miss Ellen opened her mouth, but no words came out. Clearly, she did not have anything to say. Arthur had just been proven right. It did not matter what she had said to him before, she did not see him for himself.

Just like everyone else, she assumed he was exactly like his father. How was he ever going to spread his wings and show the world he was a different person? How was he ever going to be himself?

"I shall take my leave right away." Arthur bowed to Miss Ellen for politeness, which only made them feel even more like strangers. The closeness they had built up between them had dissipated. It broke his heart. He really cared for Miss Ellen. He truly did love her.

But if she could not love him, then where did that leave them?

He turned on his heels and stalked off, each step making his heart sink even more. How had things gone so terribly wrong?

Of course, deep down, he already knew the answer to that. The moment Arthur told his father that he did not wish to exchange the Greenfield land for Miss Ellen's hand in marriage, he knew something terrible was going to happen. He hadn't imagined it would be this, though. He had not thought the duke would go so far to end his engagement. What was worse was that it had worked.

Arthur did not see the other sisters on his journey to the carriage, which was probably for the best because he did not know what he would have said to them. He just wanted to climb into the carriage and not see anyone ever again.

His mood did not improve as the carriage took him home. He remained sour, with his arms folded across his chest and his head low. He did not know who his anger was directed at more. His father, who had caused all this trouble, or Miss Ellen, who had seemingly discarded him so easily.

By the time Arthur reached the Maxwell estate, he was ready to fight with his father to ensure he got all the answers he so desperately needed. He stormed inside the building, heading straight for his father's office. He knew that if the duke was at home, that was where he would be.

And he was right. Behind his desk, buried in paperwork, sat the duke. His presence irritated Arthur, as he did not look troubled at all by what he had done. How could he not be affected by his behavior?

"Father, we must talk," Arthur declared. He did not wish to be pushed to one side and ignored until the duke was ready. "We must talk right away. I have to know what you have done to Miss Ellen."

His father did not look up for a while. He continued to write for a moment, clearly to annoy Arthur. It worked.

"Yes, Arthur," he eventually replied with a terrible smugness. "What are you here for? Something to do with Miss Ellen?"

"You know exactly what I am talking about," Arthur snapped back. "The horse. What have you done with the horse? Because she is so terribly upset."

"A horse?" The duke pursed his lips as if in deep thought. "I do not know what you are talking about. I think it is time for you to go."

"No, I am not leaving." Arthur shook his head ferociously. He was not going to be bullied by his father anymore. Not over this. "I need to know what you have done."

Arthur's heart beat a little bit faster as the duke rose to his feet with a glaring anger flashing in his eyes. This was bad; it was definitely going to be dreadful.

"You should not get involved with things you do not understand."

"I just want to know the truth," Arthur demanded.

"You cannot cope with the truth. That is why I am not telling you—"

"I am no longer a child. I can handle anything."

The duke narrowed his eyes and examined Arthur as if he were an idiot. "You can't seem to see through this Miss Ellen, so I am not too sure about that. You have not been able to see through her at all."

"She has not lied to me. Not at all." Arthur shook his head, but it made no difference to his father. The duke was unaffected.

"You do not think it is strange that she is more concerned about some fields than her sisters are?" The duke cocked an eyebrow. "That she has no real concern for her family's wishes at all? Because I think that is off-putting—"

The words sounded as if they might have come from Miss Gracelyn. She had clearly been whispering into his father's ears and making him believe things that were not true. How could Arthur overcome that? The duke had stars in his eyes when it came to Miss Gracelyn. He seemed to think that just because she was beautiful and young, that she could do no wrong.

Miss Gracelyn was far more troublesome than Miss Ellen could ever be.

"I do not know what you mean—"

"Yes, you do, Arthur. Do not be silly."

Arthur's chest tightened. The words that Miss Ellen had yelled at him when she put the wedding off because the horse had vanished came flooding back. She really had given him the same impression that his father had just stated.

Were the land and the horse so much more important than anyone else?

Almost as soon as that thought crossed his brain, he shook it out. No. She was a sweet and loving woman. She had even confessed her love for him first. That had to mean something.

"Where is the horse?" Arthur demanded. "I need to know."

The duke smirked once more, and shook his head. "I think you need to forget about this horse now and focus on what is important."

"This is important to me."

But Arthur's words fell on deaf ears. The duke was already on his way out of the office, tutting and muttering under his breath the entire time. Arthur did not need to hear the words to know what was being spoken. There were disparaging comments about him. But Arthur could not care less about that. The horse was more important to him. If he did not find the horse, then Miss Ellen would never forgive him and see him for who he really was.

That would be the worst thing that could ever happen to him.

CHAPTER 36

EVEN JOY WAS AVOIDING ELLEN, which was terrible. She had not seen her youngest sister all morning, which was unusual. They often had breakfast together, but Joy was embroiled in the sort of boring tasks she would normally avoid.

Ellen had been forced to eat alone as Joy tended to the land just outside the window. Somehow, that made her feel even lonelier.

It made sense to Ellen that Gracelyn might not want to be around her. Their relationship had never been great, and it had been getting increasingly worse ever since their father had passed away. But with Joy . . . well, her youngest sister had always been on her side. So, their distance was heartbreaking, and Ellen knew it was all her own fault.

Ellen sighed to herself as she walked through the house, drowning in her own misery. She knew she had caused this all with her stupid plan. If she had not decided to pretend to be mad to try to push the marquess away, then none of this would be happening.

"Why did I think it was such a good idea?" she muttered to herself under her breath. "What on earth was I thinking? How did I ever come up with this stupid plan to begin with?"

It was because the idea had come to her in the middle of the night when she had not slept well. No good idea could be formed in that sort of situation. She should have known better at the time. How on earth did she get so carried away with it? Of course, she had not known about the marquess's mother at the time, but that only made things so much worse.

"My behavior was awful," she said to herself as she wandered back into her bedroom. She kept ending up back in this room because she did not have anywhere else to go. Ellen did not feel comfortable going outside when she knew her sisters were avoiding her. "It is absolutely unforgivable. I can hardly believe what I have done."

She sat back on her bed with tears brimming in her eyes. The remorse she felt for her lies and the way that she had acted was nearly overwhelming. She was not even sure if she could tell the truth anymore. It had gone too far. Now that she actually wanted to get married to the marquess, even if she had told him otherwise to his face, her plan had worked too well. Now, he was going to hate her.

"What now?" Her head fell into her hands. Dismay crushed her. "What do I do from here? Without my father, there is no one I can talk to."

Ellen wished she could just disappear. That way she could stop herself from hurting everyone. She had caused trouble for her sisters; she had created nothing but pain for Arthur. He was a sweet and compassionate man. He was also innocent in this crime. Just because his father had done something to her horse did not mean Arthur was involved.

Deep down, she knew that. The rational part of her brain had always understood it, but her mouth had gotten carried away, and she had now pushed him far away. She had been hurtful and vile, putting their wedding on the line like that! Making it a prize to be won if he returned with the horse. Even as she'd said it, Ellen had hated herself. Now, after a night of fitful rest, she hated herself even more.

"I have to fix things," she moaned to herself with her hands over her eyes. "But how? How can I make it better?"

It truly did feel horrible, hopeless, endless. Ellen knew that if she ever wanted to get married to Arthur, she must act now. She had to do something before it was too late.

Perhaps if she could find a way to expose the duke for what he had done, that might help. If she could show everyone what he had done with her horse, that would change things, wouldn't it? It might not make Arthur forgive her, but she was quite sure it would at least show she had not wrongly accused the duke.

She had considered writing Arthur a letter of apology, but she had no idea where to begin. How could she explain herself in writing? Everything was far too complex for that.

But at least it would be action. Ellen had to do something. She could not just continue to lie there all day long, moping and feeling sorry for herself. It was not making her feel very good, and it was not productive.

But how could she do it? How could she make sure she got the answer she so desperately needed? Exposing the duke would not be easy. He was a strong and powerful man with a lot of money. She did not have much to fight with.

But Ellen was going to have to try. The duke was a direct man; he always said exactly what he seemed to be thinking, even if no one else was interested. Perhaps she was going to have to act in the same manner. She needed to go to the Maxwell estate and face the duke head-on. The good thing was that she had truth on her side.

"It was definitely him," she reassured herself. "There is no one else."

It took Ellen a little while to gather up the strength to push herself up off the bed, but eventually she did. She headed outside to get the carriage ready to take her to the Maxwell estate. Ellen took a moment to look around to see if she could catch sight of her sisters, to tell them where she was going, but they were nowhere to be seen. Still avoiding her, it seemed. But if she could prove herself right, then maybe she would be able to repair those relationships as well?

Without telling anyone anything, she took the carriage to the Maxwell estate, hoping desperately that the confrontation would go well. Ellen kept trying to plan what she was going to say to the duke to get the truth out of him. It would be terrifying to imagine any lady facing a man like the duke, but what else could she do? There was no choice in the matter.

"Wait—" All of a sudden, she heard something. "What was that? What was that sound? What the—?"

Ellen asked the coachman to stop as she leaned out to see what was happening. Her heart was pounding in her throat as she spotted what she had suspected but did not wish to hope, just to have it dashed.

"Arthur!" she exclaimed. "It is you."

But it was not just the marquess who had caught her attention. It was her horse as well. Arthur was riding upon Ellen's stolen horse, heading towards the Greenfield estate, bringing him back to her. Even with her terrible behavior, he was still bringing her lovely horse back to her, which just proved how wonderful he was. She knew it, but she had allowed herself to behave deplorably.

With sheer joy radiating through her, Ellen dived out of the carriage and raced towards Arthur. After a few moments petting the horse and reacquainting herself with him, she turned back to the marquess with a soft smile.

"Thank you so much, Arthur," she declared, joy, happiness, and relief flowing through her veins. Ellen's excitement grew so much that she threw her arms around him, hugging him tight. "I can't believe you found him."

Arthur stiffened at first, but soon relaxed into the hug. The warmth of his body rested against Ellen and made her smile so much brighter. It felt so wonderful to have him in her arms, to know he did not hate her.

"I was on the way to bring your horse back to you. I found him on an abandoned estate my father recently acquired."

"You did?" Ellen leaned back and smiled at Arthur. "Thank you so much for finding him for me. I appreciate it very much. You have no idea."

There was still tension clinging to the air. Ellen knew she could dispel it by apologizing for the way that had acted beforehand. But she could not seem to quite find the words. She was lost in the marquess's eyes instead.

He was a truly beautiful man. His lovely personality shone through, and made him even more handsome. Ellen knew she could not lose him. She had to find a way to make sure that he still wanted to marry her somehow.

No wonder she loved him. No wonder she had fallen for him, despite her best efforts not to. Ellen stood no chance, and now she wanted to win him back.

Eventually she broke off their hug and stepped away from him. The cogs in her brain were spinning around at the speed of light as she tried to find the words to make things all right once more.

CHAPTER 37

ARTHUR STARED into the ocean of Miss Ellen's eyes. Clearly she wanted to tell him something, but Arthur decided to take control of the conversation for her.

"I would never lie to you, Miss Ellen," he promised. "I would also never do a thing to hurt you. I would certainly not tell you that I love you if I did not mean it. I am terribly sorry for the way that I behaved before."

"No, no, no." Miss Ellen held up her hands to silence Arthur. "You do not need to apologize. I was the one in the wrong. The things I said were absolutely unforgivable. Putting the wedding on the line until the horse was found was just ludicrous. I don't know what I was thinking."

Arthur stepped forwards and laced his hands through hers. He might have been angry and hurt at the time, but while on the hunt for the horse he had been given time to realize what had been going on. His father had done something truly terrible to Miss Ellen; he had taken away her last link to her father, so he could not blame her for her extreme display of grief.

"My father did that to you," he reassured her. "I do not blame you."

"I wish you would not be so understanding." She choked back a sob. "I have judged you harshly. I have been using my father's love of the land to mask my own selfishness. I have been a truly terrible person."

Arthur hated the way his brain automatically scanned back to his father's words. He could not imagine Miss Ellen was terrible, but he was a little worried. Especially since Miss Ellen's face grew heavy with emotions.

"What is wrong?" he asked as he took her back into his arms. "You can tell me anything. Everything and anything you want to say, please tell me. I will not judge you; I will not think less of you. Nothing you could say would make me think ill of you."

Arthur knew deep down it was the truth. He could not imagine there was anything Miss Ellen could say to put him off her. He truly had fallen in love with her. He loved her so much, he could not wait until the moment they were married. He was so thrilled that, one day, he would be able to call her his wife.

Miss Ellen leaned her head close to him, resting it on his chest, close to his heart. He wondered if she could hear it pounding.

"Arthur, I have been lying to you," she managed to breathe out. "I did not mean for things to be this way. I did not mean for things to get so out of hand. I just panicked about having to get married so soon after losing my father. I did not know what else to do, so I pretended to be a little —mad."

"I see..." Arthur was not quite sure what to say. He needed a to think about it.

"If I had known about what had happened to your mother, I would never have lied or shown such disrespect. I feel so terrible about it."

She pulled back to look him in the eyes. Arthur could see the pain brimming in her piercing green eyes. He reached out and tucked a stray strand of bright-red hair behind her ear as a soft smile spread across his face.

In a low voice, Arthur said, "I knew that in my heart. I always knew you were not mad. I could see it in your lovely green eyes. The truth can always be seen in your eyes. I knew it, I just was not sure why."

"It was not because of you," Miss Ellen said rapidly. "It was just because I was so truly afraid of everything. I was confused and stuck."

"I know, I know," Arthur did his best to reassure her. "I understand. As I said, I understand grief. I know how painful it can be."

It was far easier for Arthur to forgive Miss Ellen than he had thought it might be. He brushed his fingers along her cheek, staring into her eyes longingly, feeling his soul reaching out to grasp hers. He felt he could truly see her now. He could see her in a way he had never been able to before.

The more that he saw of Miss Ellen, the deeper he fell for her.

"I really do love you, Ellen," Arthur whispered.

"I love you too," she replied softly. "So very much."

He knew this had already been said, but this time, he wanted to do things the right way. Arthur dropped down on to one knee and pulled out the small box containing his mother's ring. It was all he had left of her, and he knew she would be so happy for him to pass it on to the woman he loved.

"Miss Ellen Greenfield, would you marry me?" he asked her thickly. "Because I would love nothing more than for you to be my wife."

Miss Greenfield's eyes grew watery with emotion. "Of course. I would love to be your wife. I can't imagine anything more wonderful."

He slipped the ring onto her finger, amazed at how perfect it looked on her hand. Yes, this was perfect. This was the start to their happy ever after.

The next time Arthur crashed his lips to hers, it was stronger than before. Finally, Arthur felt seen for who he really was. He knew Miss Ellen understood he was not his father. He felt she had known that for a very long time, but now she was finally accepting it. She was letting him in, just as he was her. They might have been strangers once upon a time, but that felt like a lifetime ago. Arthur could not remember a time when Ellen was not in his life.

But now, he could not imagine what life would be like without her. He did not even wish to picture it. He knew he would do anything to make sure nothing got in their way again. Whatever it took, they were meant to be.

Thankfully, he did not have to worry about life without her now. She had agreed to marry him at last. Officially, she was his, and he was hers.

"Come on, let us get your horse back to where he is meant to be," Arthur declared. "I think he will be happy to be back on his own land."

"Me too," Miss Ellen agreed. "Thank you very much."

She held his hand for a while, smiling at him, before they started to move back towards the Greenfield estate, and Arthur's heart kept on pounding wildly.

Yes, he was most definitely in love.

What is happening? Arthur thought to himself as he stepped back through the doors to his home. There was something strange in the air, something new in the atmosphere he could not quite fathom. It was an instinctive feeling that he could not quite shake off.

"Hello?" he called out nervously, his voice echoing through the house. "Is anybody here? I am home now."

Arthur did not usually announce himself as he stepped foot into his home, but today felt different. Perhaps it was because he had gone against his father's wishes and found Miss Ellen's horse. Not only that, but he'd taken it back to her. His father was not going to be happy when he found out what Arthur had done.

But it was very unlikely that he had found out already. The horse had been in an abandoned field, not the sort of place the duke would go. Unless he suspected what Arthur had done, of course.

Arthur continued to move through the house, even though his anxiety rose. He did not know what mood he was going to find his father in, but he knew he was going to have to face it some time. Why not do it right away, while he was feeling stronger? His talk with Miss Ellen and his kiss with her had bolstered him and made him feel so much better.

"Oh!" But it was not his father Arthur ended up walking into. It was a strange gentleman carrying a doctor's bag. "Excuse me, I am sorry. I did not know that my father had guests. I do not wish to get in the way."

"I am not exactly a guest, my lord. I am here to check on your father's health."

"My father's health?" Arthur blinked a few times as he tried to tke that in. He could hardly understand what was being said. "What do you mean?"

"Your father is terribly sick, my lord. Did you not know?"

Arthur could not be hearing the man correctly. His father never seemed sick. He did not ever look like a man who was suffering from anything. But then, the doctor would not be here for no reason. It felt like the world was spinning around Arthur, the floor was not steady underneath him. He continued to stare at the doctor, but the man had become a blur. There was even a moment when the doctor seemed to speak to him, but he could not hear a word.

His whole world had shrunk down to a small space. It was as if he had been trapped in a bubble and nothing could come in and affect him. Nothing could make him feel any better, and nothing could make him feel any worse.

"My—my father is sick?" Arthur repeated, but the words seemed to be floating in the air around him, not quite coming from his own mouth. "I do not understand."

CHAPTER 38

"THERE HAVE BEEN NO SYMPTOMS," Arthur heard himself say again. "I do not understand. What could possibly be wrong with him?"

The doctor continued to answer, but Arthur could still not hear a word. All he could think of was that his father had seemed so well. He had not shown any sign of being sick, which was so strange. The only way he could deal with it was to see his father face to face. He needed to see it for himself.

"Father?" Arthur ran to the duke's bedchambers. "Father, what is this?"

By the time Arthur reached his father, he was in for a shock. The man he had seen working so hard at his desk only a short time ago now looked colorless and tired.

"You are sick?" he demanded, stepping inside the room. "How long has this been going on? How could I not know about this?"

"Why do you think I have been trying to teach you our business?" the duke replied weakly. "Why do you think I have been pushing so hard for this arrangement with the King? I want to leave you well prepared."

Arthur's heart sank. So, this truly was happening? His father really was sick. It pained him; it was almost as if he had been punched in the stomach. His whole world was about to be turned on its head.

"I do not understand." Arthur sank to his knees by his father's bed.

"I knew you would be upset, which is why I kept it from you."

There were so many things Arthur wanted to say, but the words seemed to be stuck in his throat. He might have lost his mother, but it had never really occurred to him that he would have to lose his father one day as well.

"You really are sick then?" he checked, needing it confirmed yet again.

"I am," the duke agreed. "And I probably do not have much time. I might not have fulfilled all the promises I wanted to, such as the arrangement with the King, but I have done what I can to ensure you have everything in place."

"What do you mean?" Arthur's head was still spinning. "I do not need the King. I do not need the business. I do not want anything to happen to you."

He might not have always gotten along well with his father, but that did not mean he wanted to lose him. Then he would have nothing, he would have no one—just like Ellen. She had no parent left either.

"All the paperwork has been signed," the duke continued, almost as if Arthur had not spoken, but his voice was a lot weaker than before. "You have this estate, and all the others. That means you can also do whatever you want with the Greenfield fields as well. I have concluded that I can't control what you do next. That is all up to you. If the deal with the King is not as important to you as it is me, then that is fine."

It was the most genuine that Arthur had ever heard his father say. He really did seem to care about making his son happy, which only made this whole experience so much more heartbreaking. If only they had been able to communicate so easily before his father had become ill!

Arthur was choked with emotion. It was not going to be easy to express his feelings, but he knew that this might be one of the few chances he would get to do so. Since his father had declined so rapidly, he did not know how much time he had left.

"I might not have always shown it," he said, his voice shuddering, "but I am very grateful for how hard you have worked to give me the best life possible. Things might not have always been straightforward between us, but I appreciate you, Father."

"You have not always seemed as if you agree with my way of doing things," the duke replied, but he had a small smile on his face.

"No, you are right." Arthur sniffed and nodded. "I have not always agreed with the things you have done. You have not always made the decisions I would have made, but that does not mean I have no respect for you. I am very respectful of your business and the way you have handled your duties as a duke, a landowner and a businessman."

"Do not talk about me in the past tense just yet," the duke chuckled. "I will still be doing as much business as I can. There is still some life in me yet."

Arthur choked back his feelings. It was all so sudden and hard to digest, but he was doing his best not to lose his mind; he wanted to show his father some strength. He decided to let his father make his joke.

"Well, that is good news. The business needs you."

"I think you might be the one who needs me," he laughed back. "But if you would still like to, I will continue to train you on the business side of things. That way, you have the option of continuing with it if you wish to."

It had never been what Arthur wanted, but now his father was in such a precarious, dangerous position, it did not seem so important. He could at the very least learn the full ins and outs of the business. It could be a good experience for them both. "Yes, I would like that."

"That is wonderful." Arthur could not help but notice how the old man's eyes lit up. He had never seen his father want to get close to him before this. "But we shall have to do it soon. Just in case, you understand? I suppose I have been sick for a while."

Arthur swallowed hard. "How long?"

The duke slid his eyes closed. "Probably too long. It does not really matter now. But it means I shall get to be with your mother again soon."

Arthur did not know what he was saying, not until the words fell passed his lips. "Father, what really happened to Mother? It was not sickness, was it?"

He knew what the answer was going to be, but that did not make it any less shocking to see his father shake his head. "No, that is not what happened. In fact, I only let you believe as much to protect you. I did not think you would want to hear that her mental health took a toll and she ended up taking her own life."

Arthur swallowed hard again. That was a lot for him to hear. This whole day had been a lot for him to cope with. "I suspected as much. Thank you for trying to protect me, though. I think it was probably for the best when I was younger."

"But you have grown into an adult now. I might not have always acted like it, but I have enjoyed watching you grow. Whether you decide to go forth with the business or not, I know you will do well in life. I am also sure that if you do decide to marry Miss Ellen, then you will be a great husband—and father."

"Do you think I should marry her?" Arthur felt compelled to ask. "Because I have been very confused about your feelings towards her."

The duke huffed heavily, as if he was not quite sure how to express his feelings. "I have not always been convinced that she is right for you, but that might be because I have been more focused on her land than her as a person. I have been trying to push for the alliance with the King, so I have not been thinking about you so much. The more important question is, what do you think about her?"

Arthur paused for a moment. He needed to make sure his answer was the right one. "I think I have been falling in love with her."

The duke smiled, almost to himself, and nodded. "I thought as much. I might have been trying to push you away from her because I did not think you would get what you wanted from her. But now I can see the land does not matter to you. It never has. I have actually seen a change in you while you have been with her. So, do you think you are going to be happy with her? Do you think you will have a good life together? Will you be a family?"

Arthur nodded, but his eyes welled up. He realized his father would likely not be around to see any of that. If the duke was as sick as it seemed, then he would not be alive for too much longer. Neither of his parents would get to see his wedding, or any family to follow. The same could be said for Miss Ellen's parents as well. That was a very sad thought.

Tears started to stream down his face. He could not hold it in anymore. "I do not want you to leave me," he begged. "I am not ready for that."

"Like I said, Son, I will hang around for as long as I can. I still want to help you with the business. I want you to have as much information as possible, so you can have the best life possible."

"Will you be here for the wedding?"

"I do not know," the duke confessed. "The doctor does not have much hope. But you know me, I am a very determined man."

Arthur's heart broke that little bit more. His father was strong and powerful, but he could still die soon. The future Arthur had pictured had been turned on its head.

EPILOGUE

ELLEN STARED at Gracelyn's bedroom door, wondering if she should knock to see how her sister was faring. But she was not sure what Gracelyn's mood would be today. She had been very temperamental since the duke had passed away. His death was not unexpected, but Gracelyn's reaction was.

"Ellen, I have been searching for you." Ellen's thoughts were distracted by Joy standing by her side. "Are you still worried about Gracelyn?"

Ellen nodded and shrugged her shoulders. "I just had no idea that Gracelyn had such strong feelings for the duke. I am shocked."

"I spent a lot of time with Gracelyn yesterday. I do not think she had romantic feelings for the duke. I believe it is more a sense of general loss," Joy reasoned. "I also believe that the marquess losing both of his parents too has made her really deal with the grief of us having suffered the same thing. She never really dealt with Father's death when it happened. She was too busy lashing out at everyone, so now—"

Ellen hung her head low. She felt sorry for her sister. Gracelyn had become quieter and more reserved in recent times, so Joy's words made a lot of sense. But the pain of grief was so acute, she would not wish it on anyone.

"Do not worry," Joy reassured her while rubbing her back. "This will be good for Gracelyn. It is a horrible thing that she is going through, but it will bring her to a better place in the end. She will become herself once more. Remember what she used to be like? I know she has always been argumentative, but she has not always been such hard work. There was a time when we all got along well."

Before Ellen could answer, Gracelyn's bedroom door clicked open, shocking the pair of them. The girls all froze. Neither knew what to say.

"Have you been worried about me?" Gracelyn finally asked, breaking the silence. "I am sorry, I did not mean to make you worry. I might have been sad, but I am going to focus more on gaining and not losing." She pursed her lips thoughtfully. "And what I want to gain is my relationship with my sisters again."

After so much tension flooding between them for such a long time, perhaps Ellen should have been a little more wary of Gracelyn. But to be honest, this was all she wanted as well. Her life had been changing over the last year, and it was about to change a whole lot more. She wanted to start that life with everything in her home settled. She wanted her sisters to be by her side.

Ellen opened her arms and invited her sister in for a hug. Gracelyn looked a little bewildered by the gesture, but eventually, she gave in and fell against Ellen. It was emotional for the pair of them, a moment that had been a long time coming. Ellen felt like Gracelyn was as happy as she was to have the relationship repaired. Or, at the very least, on the way to being repaired.

"We can't hug all day," Gracelyn finally laughed while sniffing, as she pulled back. "We have a wedding to get on with. You are not even dressed yet, Ellen. I can't believe it—you are the bride! Come on, I will help you."

"Me too!" Joy joined in, reminding them both that she was there. "You know, Father would be so proud of you both. Mother would be so proud of your spirit and dedication, and you know they would both love to be here now."

Ellen's heart skipped a few beats. She had not ever wanted to get married without her father there to see it, but she had no choice anymore. She could only be happy that he would have given her relationship his blessing.

Perhaps she had not had a picture book meeting with Arthur—now Duke of York—she had to remember that, but somehow through all of it, she had fallen head over heels in love. She had everything she'd ever wanted for her marriage.

Now she had been courted for a year, and she knew him inside and out. Just as he did her. She might not be perfect, but he did not mind. He adored her anyway, which was perfect. She did not know she could feel so safe and loved. Ellen could not wait to finally be married to him forever.

"Will you help me get dressed?" Ellen asked her sisters with tears in her eyes. They were half-happy tears because this was going to be the best day of her life, and she had both Joy and Gracelyn with her, which was truly unexpected. But there were sad tears as well because her father was not going to be there.

"Of course, we will help you," Gracelyn insisted. "We are both very excited about the day. We want you to look as beautiful as possible."

Ellen could not wait to get into her wedding dress. The duke had actually insisted on buying her an expensive wedding dress before he passed away, because he wanted to do his part for the wedding. It had been specially made just for her. It was gorgeous and fit her very well, showing off her figure perfectly. The expensive material covered in lace made her look just like the princess she had always wanted to be. Only she was not going to be a princess; instead, she would be a duchess.

Ellen could not picture herself as a duchess. It seemed very strange for her to have a title, but here she was, living a life she had never thought she would have, and it was wonderful. Especially now she had Gracelyn back on her side.

~

"Oh," Ellen gasped as she saw the gorgeous church display organized just for her wedding. "It looks stunning."

The church was illuminated by the sun, which only made her pulse race even faster with excitement. With her sisters by her side, in their lovely lilac gowns, knowing that she was going to see her soon-to-be husband in just moments, Ellen was on top of the world.

"Come on," Gracelyn giggled. "Let us go inside. It is time to get married after all. Unless you are thinking about running off into the sunset?"

Ellen shot her sister a look. She knew Gracelyn was being playful, but she would never run from Arthur. She had been wanting to marry him for far too long.

"I would like to get married, even if I am a little nervous."

"You do not need to be nervous. We are here for you always."

As they walked into the church, all eyes turned to look at them. But Ellen did not notice any of them. She was aware of them, but the only eyes she could spot were Arthur's. He was staring at her as if she was the most beautiful woman on the planet, which was only highlighted by the wedding theme of everlasting love—something that felt truly right for herself and Arthur.

"What is mine will always be yours," Arthur had told her not so long ago. "Once we are married, we shall share everything. Except for the fields. And your horse as well, of course. They will always be yours. I will never take them from you, ever."

That was the sweetest thing that anyone could have ever said to her. Ellen knew in that moment she was making the right move. This was the man she needed to be with forever, and those words stuck with her as she moved down the aisle to meet him. This was the moment she was going to become his wife, which was truly thrilling. She almost wanted to run towards him. If her sisters were not beside her, keeping her calm and under control, then she might well have done.

"You look beautiful," Arthur whispered as soon as she was within listening distance. "You really are the loveliest woman I have ever met. I am so lucky."

Ellen giggled as heat rose to her cheeks and she tucked a stray strand of hair behind her ear. "Well, you look utterly handsome as well. I think I am the lucky one."

It was true. He really did look very handsome in his suit. Of course, the moment was bitter-sweet, as neither of them had their parents there to witness their ceremony, but at least they were not alone.

Ellen felt she was not alone any more. He might not have been here in person, but she could have sworn that her father's presence was surrounding her. It was truly the closest she had felt to him since he'd passed away. Not because she was pretending that he was a horse, but because it really did seem as if he had his arms around her, comforting her and letting her know that all would be well from there on. She had not lost anything, she was simply gaining something new.

Who would have thought that Gracelyn would have come up with such wise words? It seemed that everything was changing for the better.

The couple still had a lot of love in their lives, and that was only about to increase as Ellen married this wonderful man and became Duchess of York. Arthur slipped his hands into hers, and they held onto each other, staring lovingly into one another's eyes as the priest began to speak, saying the wonderful, traditional vows that would bind them together forever. The words Ellen had been practicing every single night before she went to sleep, so she could make sure she got them right.

This was the start of the rest of Ellen's life, and she could not wait to for it to begin. This was her happily ever after, and it was going to be wonderful.

EXTENDED EPILOGUE

I am humbled you finished reading my novel *"From Denial to Desire"*.

Are you aching to know what happens to our lovebirds?

Click on the image or the link below to connect to a more personal level and as a BONUS, I will send you the Extended Epilogue of this Book!

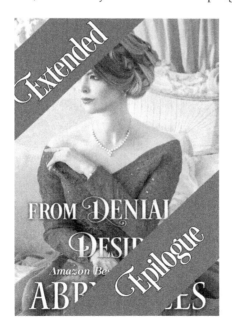

UNTITLED

A MESSAGE FROM ABBY

Dear Reader,

Thank you for reading! I hope you enjoyed every page and I would love to hear your thoughts whether it be a review online or you contact me via my website. I am eternally grateful for you and none of this would be possible without our shared love of romance.

I pray that someday I will get to meet each of you and thank you in person, but in the meantime, all I can do is tell you how amazing you are.

As I prepare my next love story for you, keep believing in your dreams and know that mine would not be possible without you.

With Love,

Abby Ayles

ABOUT STARFALL PUBLICATIONS

Starfall Publications has helped me and so many others extend my passion from writing to you.

The prime focus of this company has been – and always will be – *quality* and I am honored to be able to publish my books under their name.

Having said that, I would like to officially thank Starfall Publications for offering me the opportunity to be part of such a wonderful, hard-working team!

Thanks to them, my dreams – and your dreams — have come true!

ABOUT ABBY AYLES

Abby Ayles was born in the northern city of Manchester, England, but currently lives in Charleston, South Carolina, with her husband and their three cats. She holds a Master's degree in History and Arts and worked as a history teacher in middle school.

Her greatest interest lies in the era of Regency and Victorian England and Abby shares her love and knowledge of these periods with many readers in her newsletter.

In addition to this she has also written her first romantic novel, *The Duke's Secrets*, which is set in the era and is available for free on her website. As one reader commented *"Abby's writing makes you travel back in time!"*

When she has time to herself, Abby enjoys going to the theatre, reading and watching documentaries about Regency and Victorian England.

Social Media

- Facebook
- Goodreads
- Amazon
- BookBub

ALSO BY ABBY AYLES

- The Lady, The Duke and The Gentleman
- A Broken Heart's Redemption
- Falling for the Governess
- The Lady's Gamble
- The Lady's Patient
- Saving Lady Abigail
- Engaging Love
- Portrait of Love
- A Mysterious Governess for the Reluctant Earl
- Loving A Lady
- Entangled with the Duke
- The Secret to the Ladies' Hearts
- Falling for the Hartfield Ladies
- Capturing the Viscount's Heart
- The Odd Mystery of the Cursed Duke
- Secret Dreams of a Fearless Governess
- A Second Chance for the Tormented Lady
- The Lady in the Gilded Cage
- The Mysteries of a Lady's Heart
- A Daring Captain for her Loyal Heart
- The Earl's Wager for a Lady's Heart
- Melting a Duke's Winter Heart
- A Guiding Light for the Lost Earl
- A Loving Duke for the Shy Duchess
- The Earl Behind the Mask
- Freed by The Love of an Earl
- The Lady of the Lighthouse
- Chronicles of Regency Love

- Inconveniently Betrothed to an Earl
- A Forbidden Gamble for the Duke's Heart
- A Muse for the Lonely Marquess
- Broken Hearts and Doting Earls
- A Forbidden Bid for the Lady's Heart
- A Healer for the Marquess' Heart
- A Reluctant Bride for the Baron
- A Forbidden Love for the Rebellious Baron
- How to Train a Duke in the Ways of Love
- Caught in the Storm of a Duke's Heart
- A Christmas Worth Remembering
- Unlocking the Secrets of a Duke's Heart
- Reforming the Rigid Duke
- What the Governess is Hiding
- Betrayal and Redemption
- Fateful Twists and Unexpected Loves
- Stealing Away the Governess
- A Tale of Two Sisters
- Desire and Fear
- Fateful Romances in the Most Unexpected Places
- Marriage by Mistake
- The Secret of a Lady's Heart
- The Lady's Right Option
- A Lady's Forgiveness
- The Ladies, The Dukes and Their Secrets

Printed in Great Britain
by Amazon

14044186R00119